Behind the Green Door

Mildred A. Wirt

Pharos Books

ISBN: 978-93-55464-24-8
eISBN: 978-93-55464-44-6

©Publisher

Publisher: Pharos Books (P) Ltd.
Plot No.-63, 1st Floor, Main Mother Dairy Road
Pandav Nagar, East Delhi-110092
Phone: 011-40395855, +4049916623
WhatsApp: +91 8368220032
E-mail: sales@pharosbooks.in
Website: www.pharosbooks.in
First Edition: 2024

Behind the Green Door
Mildred A. Wirt

CONTENTS

CHAPTER 1

TROUBLE FOR MR. PARKER

"Watch me coming down the mountain, Mrs. Weems! This one is a honey! An open christiana turn with no brakes dragging!"

Penny Parker, clad in a new black and red snowsuit, twisted her agile young body sideways, causing the small rug upon which she stood to skip across the polished floor of the living room. She wriggled her slim hips again, and it slipped in the opposite direction toward Mrs. Weems who was watching from the kitchen doorway.

"Coming down the mountain, my eye!" exclaimed the housekeeper, laughing despite herself. "You'll be coming down on your head if you don't stop those antics. I declare, you've acted like a crazy person ever since your father rashly agreed to take you to Pine Top for the skiing."

"I have to break in my new suit and limber up my muscles somehow," said Penny defensively. "One can't practice outdoors when there's no snow. Now watch this one, Mrs. Weems. It's called a telemark."

"You'll reduce that rug to shreds before you're through," sighed the housekeeper. "Can't you think of anything else to do?"

"Yes," agreed Penny cheerfully, "but it wouldn't be half as much fun. How do you like my suit?" She darted across the room to preen before the full length mirror.

A red-billed cap pulled at a jaunty angle over her blond curls, Penny made a striking figure in the well tailored suit of dark wool. Her eyes sparkled with the joy of youth and it was easy for her to smile. She was an only child, the daughter of Anthony Parker, editor and publisher of the *Riverview Star*, and her mother had died when she was very young.

"It looks like a good, practical suit," conceded the housekeeper.

Penny made a wry face. "Is that the best you can say for it? Louise Sidell and I shopped all over Riverview to get the snappiest number out, and then you call it *practical*."

"Oh, you know you look cute in it," laughed Mrs. Weems. "So what's the use of telling you?"

Before Penny could reply the telephone rang and the housekeeper went to answer it. She returned to the living room a moment later to say that Penny's father was in need of free taxi service home from the office.

"Tell him I'll be down after him in two shakes of a kitten's tail!" Penny called, making for the stairway.

She took the steps two at a time and had climbed halfway out of the snowsuit by the time she reached the bedroom. A well aimed kick landed the garment on the bed, and then because it was very new and very choice she took time to straighten it out. Seizing a dress blindly from the closet, she wriggled into it and ran downstairs again.

"Some more skiing equipment may come while I'm gone," she shouted to Mrs. Weems who was in the kitchen. "I bought a new pair of skis, a couple of poles, three different kinds of wax and a pair of red mittens."

"Why didn't you order the store sent out and be done with it?" responded the housekeeper dryly.

Penny pulled on her heavy coat and hurried to the garage where two cars stood side by side. One was a shining black sedan of the latest model, the other, a battered, unwashed vehicle whose reputation was as discouraging as its appearance. "Leaping Lena," as Penny called her car, had an annoying habit of running up repair bills, and then repaying its long suffering owner by refusing to start on cold winter days.

"Lena, you get to stay in your cozy nest this time," Penny remarked, climbing into her father's sedan. "Dad can't stand your rattle and bounce."

   Behind the Green Door

The powerful engine started with a blast. While Mrs. Weems watched anxiously from the kitchen window, Penny shot the car out backwards, wheeling it around the curve of the driveway with speed and ease. She liked to handle her father's automobile, and since he did not enjoy driving, she frequently called at the newspaper office to take him home.

The *Star* building occupied a block in the downtown section of Riverview. Penny parked the car beside the loading dock at the rear, and took an elevator to the editorial rooms. Nearly all of the desks were deserted at this late hour of the afternoon. But Jerry Livingston, one of the best reporters on the paper, was still pecking out copy on a noisy typewriter.

"Hi, Penny!" he observed, grinning as she brushed past his desk. "Have you caught any more witch dolls?"

"Not for the front page," she flung back at him. "My newspaper career is likely to remain in a state of *status quo* for the next two weeks. Dad and I are heading for Pine Top to dazzle the natives with our particular brand of skiing. Don't you envy us?"

"I certainly would, if you were going."

"If!" exclaimed Penny indignantly. "Of course we're going! We leave Thursday by plane. Dad needs a vacation and this time I know he won't try to wiggle out of it at the last minute."

"Well, I hope not," replied Jerry in a skeptical voice. "Your father needs a good rest, Penny. But I have a sneaking notion you're in for a disappointment again."

"What makes you say that, Jerry? Dad promised me faithfully—"

"Sure, I know," he nodded, "but there have been developments."

"An important story?"

"No, it's more serious than that. But you talk with him. I may have the wrong slant on the situation."

Not without misgiving, Penny went on to her father's private office and tapped on the door.

"Come in," he called in a gruff voice, and as she entered, waved her into a chair. "You arrived a little sooner than I expected, Penny. Mind waiting a few minutes?"

"Not at all."

Studying her father's lean, tired-looking face, Penny decided that something *was* wrong. He seemed unusually worried and nervous.

"A hard day, Dad?" she asked.

Mr. Parker finished straightening a sheaf of papers before he glanced up.

"Yes, I hadn't intended to tell you until later, but I may as well. I'm afraid our trip is off—at least as far as I'm concerned."

"Oh, Dad!"

"It's a big disappointment, Penny. The truth is, I'm in a spot of trouble."

"Isn't that the usual condition of a newspaper publisher?"

"Yes," he smiled, "but there are different degrees of trouble, and this is the worst possible. The *Star* has been sued for libel, a matter of fifty odd thousand."

"Fifty thousand!" gasped Penny. "But of course you'll win the suit!"

"I'm not at all sure of it." Anthony Parker spoke grimly. "My lawyer tells me that Harvey Maxwell has a strong case against the paper."

"Harvey Maxwell?" repeated Penny thoughtfully. "Isn't he the man who owns the Riverview Hotel?"

"Yes, and a chain of other hotels and lodges throughout the country. Harvey Maxwell is a rather well known sportsman. He lives lavishly, travels a great deal, and in general is a hard, shrewd business man."

"He's made a large amount of money from his hotels, hasn't he?"

"Maxwell acquired a fortune from some source, but I've always had a doubt that it came from the hotel business."

"Why is he suing the *Star* for libel, Dad?"

   Behind the Green Door

"Early this fall, while I was out of town for a day DeWitt let a story slip through which should have been killed. It was an interview with a football player named Bill Morcrum who was quoted as saying that he had been approached by Maxwell who offered him a bribe to throw an important game."

"What would be the reason behind that?"

"Maxwell is thought by those in the know to have a finger in nearly every dishonest sports scheme ever pulled off in this town. He places heavy wagers, and seldom comes out on the losing end. But the story never should have been published."

"It was true though?"

"I'm satisfied it was," replied Mr. Parker. "However, it always is dangerous to make insinuations against a man."

"Can't the story be proven? I should think with the football player's testimony you would have a good case."

"That's the trouble, Penny. This boy, Bill Morcrum, now claims he never made any such accusation against Maxwell. He says the reporter misquoted him and twisted his statements."

"Who covered the story, Dad?"

"A man named Glower, a very reliable reporter. He swears he made no mistake, and I am inclined to believe him."

"Then why did the football player change his story?"

"I have no proof, but it's a fairly shrewd guess that he was approached by Maxwell a second time. Either he was threatened or offered a bribe which was large enough to sway him."

"With both Maxwell and the football player standing together, it does rather put you on the spot," Penny acknowledged. "What are you going to do?"

"We'll fight the case, of course, but unless we can prove that our story was accurate, we're almost sure to lose. I've asked Bill Morcrum to come to my office this afternoon, and he promised he would. He's overdue now."

Anthony Parker glanced at his watch and scowled. Getting up from the swivel chair he began to pace to and fro across the room.

A buzzer on his desk gave three sharp, staccato signals.

"Morcrum must be here now!" the editor exclaimed in relief. "I'll want to see him alone."

Penny arose to leave. As she went out the doorway she met the receptionist, accompanied by an awkward, oversized youth who shuffled his feet in walking. He grinned at her in a sheepish way and entered the private office.

While Penny waited, she entertained herself by reading all the comic strips she could find in the out-of-town exchange papers. In the adjoining room she could hear the rhythmical thumping, clicking sound of the *Star's* teletype machines. She wandered aimlessly into the room to read the copy just as the machines typed it out, a story from Washington, one from Chicago, another from Los Angeles. It was fascinating to watch the print appear like magic upon the long rolls of copy paper.

Presently, the teletype attendant, young Billy Stevens, came dashing into the room.

"Oh, hello, Miss Parker," he said with a bashful grin.

"Hello, Billy," Penny answered cordially. She studied the keyboard of the sending teletype machine, running her fingers over the letters. "I wish I could work this thing," she said.

"There's nothing to it if you can run a typewriter," answered Billy. "Just a minute, I'll throw it off the line on to the test position. Then you can try it."

At first Penny's copy was badly garbled, but under Billy's enthusiastic coaching she was soon doing accurate work.

"Say, this is fun!" she declared. "I'm coming in again one of these days and practice. Thanks a lot, Billy!"

As Penny went back into the editorial room she saw the Morcrum boy leaving her father's office. His head was downcast and his face was flushed to the ears. Obviously, he had not had a comfortable time with Mr. Parker.

Behind the Green Door

The moment the boy had vanished, Penny hurried into her father's office to learn the outcome of the interview.

"No luck," reported Mr. Parker, reaching for his hat and overcoat.

"He wouldn't change his story?"

"No. He seemed like a fairly decent sort of boy, but he kept insisting he had been misquoted. I couldn't get anywhere with him. He'll testify for Maxwell when the case comes to trial."

Mr. Parker put on his overcoat and hat, and opened the door for Penny. As they left the building he told her more about the interview.

"I asked the boy point-blank if he hadn't been hired by Maxwell. Naturally, he denied it, but he acted rather alarmed. Oh, I'm satisfied he's either been bought off or threatened."

"When does the case come to trial?"

"The last of next month, unless we gain a delay."

"That gives you quite a bit of time. Don't you think you could take two weeks off anyhow, Dad? We both planned upon having such a wonderful time at Mrs. Downey's place."

Penny and her father had been invited to spend the Christmas holidays at Pine Top, a winter resort which attracted many Riverview persons. They especially had looked forward to the trip since they were to have been the house guests of Mrs. Christopher Downey, an old friend of Mr. Parker's who operated a skiing lodge on the slopes of the mountain overlooking Silver Valley.

"There's not much chance of my getting away," Mr. Parker replied regretfully. "That is, not unless important evidence falls into my hands, or I am able to make a deal with Maxwell."

"A deal?"

"If he would make reasonable demands I might be willing to settle out of court."

Penny gazed at her father in blank amazement.

"And admit you were in the wrong when you're certain you weren't?"

"Any good general will make a strategic retreat if the situation calls for it. It might be more sensible to settle out of court than to lose the case. Maxwell has me in a tight place and knows it."

"Then why don't you see him? He might be fairly reasonable."

"I suppose I could stop at the Riverview Hotel on our way home," Mr. Parker said, frowning thoughtfully. "There's an outside chance Maxwell may come to terms. Drop me off there, Penny."

While the car threaded its way in and out of dense traffic, the editor remained in a deep study. Penny had never seen him look so worried. Her own disappointment was keen, yet she realized that far more than a vacation trip was at stake. Fifty thousand dollars represented a large sum of money! If Maxwell won his suit it might even mean the loss of the *Riverview Star*.

Sensing his daughter's alarm, Mr. Parker reached out to pat her knee.

"Don't worry," he said, "we're not licked yet, Penny! And if there's any way to arrange it, you shall have your trip to Pine Top just as we planned."

***

CHAPTER 2

A RIVAL REPORTER

Penny presently edged the sedan into a parking space across the street from the Riverview Hotel. As she switched off the ignition her father said:

"Better come along with me and wait in the lobby. It's cold out here."

Penny followed her father into the building. The hotel was an elegant one with many services available for guests. She noticed a florist shop, a candy store, a dry cleaning establishment, and even a small brokerage office opening off the lobby.

"Oh, yes," said Mr. Parker as Penny called his attention to the brokerage. "Maxwell hasn't overlooked anything. The hotel has a special leased wire which I've been told gives him a direct connection with his other places."

Walking over to the desk, Mr. Parker mentioned his name and asked the clerk if he might see Harvey Maxwell.

"Mr. Maxwell is not here," replied the man with an insolent air.

"When will he be at the hotel?"

"Mr. Maxwell has left the city on business. He does not expect to return until the end of next month."

Mr. Parker could not hide his annoyance.

"Let me have his address then," he said in a resigned voice. "I'll write him."

The clerk shook his head. "I have been instructed not to give you Mr. Maxwell's address. If you wish to deal with him you will have to see his lawyer, Gorman S. Railey."

"So Maxwell was expecting me to come here to make a deal with him?" demanded Mr. Parker. "Well, I've changed my mind. I'll make a deal all right, but it will be in court. Good day!"

Angrily, the newspaper man strode from the lobby. Penny hurried to keep pace with him.

"That settles it," he said tersely as they climbed into the sedan again. "This libel suit will be a fight to the finish. And maybe my finish at that!"

"Oh, Dad, I'm sure you'll win. But it's a pity all this had to come up just when you had planned a fine vacation. Mrs. Downey will be disappointed, too."

"Yes, she will, Penny. And there's Mrs. Weems to be thought about. I promised her a two weeks' trip while we were gone."

They drove in silence for a few blocks. As the car passed the Sidell residence, Penny's father said thoughtfully:

"I suppose I could send you out to Pine Top alone, Penny. Or perhaps you might be able to induce your chum, Louise, to go along. Would you like that?"

"It would be more fun if you went also."

"That's out of the picture now. If everything goes well I might be able to join you for Christmas weekend."

"I'm not sure Louise could go," said Penny doubtfully. "But I can find out right away."

After dinner that night, she lost no time in running over to the Sidell home. At first Louise was thrown into a state of ecstasy at the thought of making a trip to Pine Top and then her face became gloomy.

"I would love it, Penny! But it's practically a waste of words to ask Mother. We're going to my grandmother's farm in Vermont for the holidays, and I'll have to tag along."

Since grade school days the two girls had been inseparable friends. Between them there was perfect understanding and they made an excellent pair, for Louise exerted a subduing effect upon the more impulsive, excitable Penny.

   Behind the Green Door

Inactivity bored Penny, and wherever she went she usually managed to start things moving. When nothing better offered, she tried her hand at writing newspaper stories for her father's paper. Several of these reportorial experiences had satisfied even Penny's deep craving for excitement.

Three truly "big" stories had rolled from her typewriter through the thundering presses of the *Riverview Star*: Tale of the Witch Doll, The Vanishing Houseboat, and Danger at the Drawbridge. Even now, months after her last astonishing adventure, friends liked to tease her about a humorous encounter with a certain Mr. Kippenberg's alligator.

"Pine Top won't be any fun without you, Lou," Penny complained.

"Oh, yes it will," contradicted her chum. "I know you'll manage to stir up plenty of excitement. You'll probably pull a mysterious Eskimo out of a snow bank or save Santa Claus from being kidnaped! That's the way you operate."

"Pine Top is an out of the way place, close to the Canadian border. All one can do there is eat, sleep, and ski."

"You mean, that's all one is supposed to do," corrected Louise with a laugh. "But you'll run into some big story or else you're slipping!"

"There isn't a newspaper within fifty miles. No railroad either. The only way in and out of the valley is by airplane, and bob-sled, of course."

"That may cramp your style a little, but I doubt it," declared Louise. "I do wish I could go along."

The girls talked with Mrs. Sidell, but as they both had expected, it was not practical for Louise to make the trip.

"I'll come to the airport to see you off on your plane," Louise promised as Penny left the house. "You're starting Thursday, aren't you?"

"Yes, at ten-thirty unless there's bad weather. But I'll see you again before that."

All the next day Penny packed furiously. Mr. Parker was unusually busy at the office, but he bought his daughter's ticket and made all arrangements for the trip to Pine Top. Since Mrs. Weems also planned to leave Riverview the following day, the house was in a constant state of turmoil.

"I feel sorry for Dad being left here alone," remarked Penny. "He'll never make his bed, and he'll probably exist on strong coffee and those wretched raw beef sandwiches they serve at the beanery across from the *Star* office."

"I ought to give up my vacation," declared Mrs. Weems. "It seems selfish of me not to stay here."

Mr. Parker would not hear of such an arrangement, and so plans moved forward just as if his own trip had not been postponed.

"Dad, you'll honestly try to come to Pine Top for Christmas?" Penny pleaded.

"I'll do my best," he promised soberly. "I have a hunch that Harvey Maxwell may still be in town, despite what we were told at the hotel. I intend to busy myself making a complete investigation of the man."

"If I could help, I'd be tickled to stay, Dad."

"There's nothing you can do, Penny. Just go out there and have a nice vacation."

Mr. Parker had not intended to go to the office Thursday morning until after Penny's plane had departed, but at breakfast time a call came from DeWitt, the city editor, urging his presence at once. Before leaving, he gave his daughter her ticket and travelers checks.

"Now I expect to be at the airport to see you off," he promised. "Until then, good-bye."

Mr. Parker kissed Penny and hastened away. Later, Louise Sidell came to the house. Soon after ten o'clock the girls took leave of Mrs. Weems, taxiing to the airport.

"I don't see Dad anywhere," Penny remarked as the cabman unloaded her luggage. "He'll probably come dashing up just as the plane takes off."

The girls entered the waiting room and learned that the plane was "on time." Curiously, they glanced at the other passengers. Two travelers Penny immediately tagged as business men. But she was rather interested in a plump, over-painted woman whose nervous manner suggested that she might be making her first airplane trip.

While Penny's luggage was being weighed, two men entered the waiting room. One was a lean, sharp-faced individual suffering from a bad cold. The other, struck Penny as being vaguely familiar. He was a stout man, expensively dressed, and had a surly, condescending way of speaking to his companion.

"Who are those men?" Penny whispered to Louise. "Do you know them?"

Louise shook her head.

"That one fellow looks like someone I've seen," Penny went on thoughtfully. "Maybe I saw his picture in a newspaper, but I can't place him."

The two men went up to the desk and the portly one addressed the clerk curtly:

"You have our reservations for Pine Top?"

"Yes, sir. Just sign your name here." The clerk pushed forward paper and a pen.

Paying for the tickets from a large roll of greenbacks, the two men went over to the opposite side of the waiting room and sat down. Penny glanced anxiously at the clock. It was twenty minutes past ten.

A uniformed messenger boy entered the room, letting in a blast of cold air as he opened the door. He went over to the desk and the clerk pointed out the two girls.

"Now what?" said Penny in a low voice. "Maybe my trip is called off!"

The message was for her, from her father. But it was less serious than she had expected. Because an important story had "broken" it would be impossible for him to leave the office. He wished her a pleasant trip west and again promised he would bend every effort toward visiting Pine Top for Christmas.

Penny folded the message and slipped it into her purse.

"Dad won't be able to see me off," she explained to her chum. "I was afraid when DeWitt called him this morning he would be held up."

Before Louise could reply the outside door opened once more, and a girl of perhaps twenty-two who walked with a long, masculine gait, came in out of the cold. Penny sat up a bit straighter in her chair.

"Do you see what I see?" she whispered.

"Who is she?" inquired Louise curiously.

"The one and only Francine Sellberg."

"Which means nothing to me."

"Don't tell me you haven't seen her by-line in the *Riverview Record!* Francine would die of mortification."

"Is she a reporter?"

"She covers special assignments. And she is pretty good," Penny added honestly. "But not quite as good as she believes."

"Wonder what she's doing here?"

"I was asking myself that same question."

As the two girls watched, they saw Francine's cool gaze sweep the waiting room. She did not immediately notice Penny and Louise whose backs were partly turned to her. Her eyes rested for an instant upon the two men who previously had bought tickets to Pine Top, and a flicker of satisfaction showed upon her face.

Moving directly to the desk she spoke to the ticket agent in a low voice, yet loudly enough for Penny and Louise to hear.

"Is it still possible to make a reservation for Pine Top?"

"Yes, we have one seat left on the plane."

"I'll take it," said Francine.

Penny nudged Louise and whispered in her ear: "Did you hear that?"

"I certainly did. Why do you suppose she's going to Pine Top? For the skiing?"

"Unless I'm all tangled in a knot, she's after a big story for the *Record*. And I just wonder if those two mysterious-looking gentlemen aren't the reason for her trip!"

***

CHAPTER 3

TRAVELING COMPANIONS

Francine Sellberg paid for her ticket and turned so that her gaze fell squarely upon Penny and Louise. Abruptly, she crossed over to where they sat.

"Hello, girls," she greeted them breezily. "What brings you to the airport?"

As always, the young woman reporter's manner was brusque and business-like. Without meaning to offend, she gave others an impression of regarding them with an air of condescension.

"I came to see Penny off," answered Louise before her chum could speak.

"Oh, are you taking this plane?" inquired Francine, staring at Penny with quickening interest.

"I am if it ever gets here."

"Traveling alone?"

"All by my lonesome," Penny admitted cheerfully.

"You're probably only going a short ways?"

"Oh, quite a distance," returned Penny. She did not like the way Francine was quizzing her.

"Penny is going to Pine Top for the skiing," declared Louise, never guessing that her chum preferred to withhold the information.

"Pine Top!" The smile left Francine's face and her eyes roved swiftly toward the two men who sat at the opposite side of the room.

"We are to be traveling companions, I believe," remarked Penny innocently.

Francine's attention came back to the younger girl. Her eyes narrowed with suspicion.

"So you're going out to Pine Top for the skiing," she said softly.

"And you?" countered Penny.

"Oh, certainly for the skiing," retorted Francine, mockery in her voice.

"Nice of the *Record* to give you a vacation."

By this time the silver-winged transport had wheeled into position on the apron, and passengers were beginning to leave the waiting room. The two men who had attracted Penny's attention, arose and without appearing to notice the three girls, went outside.

"You don't deceive me one bit, Penny Parker," said Francine with a quick change of attitude. "I know very well why you are going to Pine Top, and it's for the same reason I am!"

"You seem to have divined all my secrets, even when I don't know them myself," responded Penny. "Suppose you tell me why I am going to Pine Top mountain?"

"It's perfectly obvious that your father sent you, But I am afraid he over-estimates your journalistic powers if he thinks you have had enough experience to handle a difficult assignment of this sort. I'll warn you right now, Penny, don't come to me for help. On this job we're rivals. And I won't tolerate any bungling or interference upon your part!"

"Nice to know just where we stand," replied Penny evenly. "Then there will be no misunderstanding or tears later on."

"Exactly. And mind you don't give any tip-off as to who I am!"

"You mean you don't care to have those two gentlemen who were here a moment ago know that you are a reporter for the *Record*."

"Naturally."

"And who are these men of mystery?"

"As if you don't know!" Francine made an impatient gesture. "Oh, why pose, Penny? This innocent act doesn't go over worth a cent."

Louise broke indignantly into the conversation. "Penny isn't posing! It's true she is going to Pine Top for the skiing and not to get a story. Isn't it?"

"Yes," acknowledged Penny unwillingly. She was sorry that her chum had put an end to the little game with Francine.

The reporter stared at the two girls, scarcely knowing whether or not to believe them.

"Why not break down and tell me the identity of our two fellow passengers?" suggested Penny.

"So you really don't know their names?" Francine flashed a triumphant smile. "Fancy that! Well, you've proven such a clever little reporter in the past, I'll allow you to figure it out for yourself. See you in Pine Top."

Turning away, the young woman went back to the desk to speak once more with the ticket man.

"Doesn't she simply drip conceit!" Louise whispered in disgust. "Did I make a mistake in letting her know that you weren't on an assignment?"

"It doesn't matter, Lou. Shall we be going out to the plane before I miss it?"

The huge streamliner stood warming up on the ribbon of cement, long tongues of flame leaping from the exhausts. Nearly all of the passengers already had taken their seats in the warm, cozy cabin.

"Good-bye, Lou," Penny said, shaking her chum's hand.

"Good-bye. Have a nice time. And don't let that know-it-all Francine get ahead of you!"

"Not if I can help it," laughed Penny.

Francine had left the waiting room and was walking with a brisk step toward the plane. Not wishing to be the last person aboard, Penny stepped quickly into the cabin. All but two seats were taken. One was at the far end of the plane, the other directly behind the two strange men.

Penny slid into the latter chair just as Francine came into the cabin. As she went down the aisle to take the only remaining seat, the reporter shot the younger girl an irritated glance.

"She thinks I took this place just to spite her!" thought Penny. "How silly!"

The stewardess, trim in her blue-green uniform, had closed the heavy metal door. The plane began to move down the ramp, away from the station's canopied entrance. Penny leaned close to the window and waved a last good-bye to Louise.

As the speed of the engines was increased, the plane raced faster and faster over the smooth runway. A take-off was not especially thrilling to Penny who often had made flights with her father. She shook her head when the stewardess offered her cotton for her ears, but accepted a magazine.

Penny flipped carelessly through the pages. Finding no story worth reading, she turned her attention to her fellow passengers. Beside her, on the right, sat the over-painted woman, her hands gripping the arm rests so hard that her knuckles showed white.

"We—we're in the air now, aren't we?" she asked nervously, meeting Penny's gaze. "I do hope I'm not going to be sick."

"I am sure you won't be," replied Penny. "The air is very quiet today."

"They tell me flying over the mountains in winter time is dangerous."

"Not in good weather with a skilful pilot. I am sure we will be in no danger."

"Just the same I never would have taken a plane if it hadn't been the only way of reaching Pine Top."

Penny turned to regard her companion with new interest. The woman was in her early forties, though she had attempted by the lavish use of make-up to appear younger. Her hair was a bleached yellow, dry and brittle from too frequent permanent waving. Her shoes were slightly scuffed, and a tight-fitting black crepe dress, while expensive, was shiny from long use.

"Oh, are you traveling to Pine Top, too?" inquired Penny. "Half the passengers on this plane must be heading for there."

"Is that where you are going?"

"Yes," nodded Penny. "I plan to visit an old friend who has an Inn on the mountain side, and try a little skiing."

"This is strictly a business trip with me," confided the woman. She had relaxed now that the transport was flying at an even keel. "I am going there to see Mr. Balantine—David Balantine. You've heard of him, of course."

Penny shook her head.

"My dear, everyone in the East is familiar with his name. Mr. Balantine has a large chain of theatres throughout the country. He produces his own shows, too. I hope to get a leading part in a new production which will soon be cast."

"Oh, I see," murmured Penny. "You are an actress?"

"I've been on the stage since I was twelve years old," the woman answered proudly. "You must have seen my name on the billboards. I am Miss Miller. Maxine Miller."

"I should like to see one of your plays," Penny responded politely.

"The truth is I've been 'at liberty' for the past year or two," the actress admitted with an embarrassed laugh. "'At liberty' is a word we show people use when we're temporarily out of work. The movies have practically ruined the stage."

"Yes, I know."

"For several weeks I have been trying to get an interview with Mr. Balantine. His secretaries would not make an appointment for me. Then quite by luck I learned that he planned to spend two weeks at Pine Top. I thought if I could meet him out there in his more relaxed moments, he might give me a role in the new production."

"Isn't it a rather long chance to take?" questioned Penny. "To go so far just in the hope of seeing this man?"

"Yes, but I like long chances. And I've tried every other way to meet him. If I win the part I'll be well repaid for my time and money."

"And if you fail?"

Maxine Miller shrugged. "The bread line, perhaps, or burlesque which would be worse. If I stay at Pine Top more than a few days I'll never have money enough to get back here. They tell me Pine Top is high-priced."

"I don't know about that," answered Penny.

As the plane winged its way in a northwesterly direction, the actress kept the conversational ball rolling at an exhausting pace. She told Penny all about herself, her trials and triumphs on the stage. As first, it was fairly interesting, but as Miss Miller repeated herself, the girl became increasingly bored. She shrewdly guessed that the actress never had been the outstanding stage success she visioned herself.

Penny paid more than ordinary attention to the two men who sat in front of her. However, Miss Miller kept her so busy answering questions that she could not have overheard their talk, even if she had made an effort to do so.

Therefore, when the plane made a brief stop, she was astonished to have Francine sidle over to her as she sat on a high stool at the lunch stand, and say in a cutting tone:

"Well, did you find out everything you wanted to know? I saw you listening hard enough."

"Eavesdropping isn't my method," replied Penny indignantly. "It's stupid and is employed only by trash fiction writers and possibly *Record* reporters."

"Say, are you suggesting—?"

"Yes," interrupted Penny wearily. "Now please go find yourself a roost!"

Francine ignored the empty stools beside Penny and went to the far side of the lunch room. A moment later the two men, who had caused the young woman reporter such concern, entered and sat down at a counter near Penny, ordering sandwiches and coffee.

Rather ironically, the girl could not avoid hearing their conversation, and almost their first words gave her an unpleasant shock.

"Don't worry, Ralph," said the stout one. "Nothing stands in our way now."

"You're not forgetting Mrs. Downey's place?"

"We'll soon take care of *her*," the other boasted. "That's why I'm going out to Pine Top with you, Ralph. I'll show you how these little affairs are handled."

***

CHAPTER 4

PINE TOP MOUNTAIN

Penny was startled by the remarks of the two men because she felt certain that the Mrs. Downey under discussion must be the woman at whose inn she would spend a two weeks' vacation. Was it possible that a plot was being hatched against her father's friend? And what did Francine know about it?

She glanced quickly toward the young woman reporter who was doing battle with a tough steak which threatened to leap off her plate whenever she tried to cut it. Apparently, Francine had not heard any part of the conversation.

Being only human, Penny decided that despite her recent comments, she could not be expected to abandon a perfectly good sandwich in the interests of theoretical honor. She remained at her post and waited for the men to reveal more.

Unobligingly, they began to talk of the weather and politics. Penny finished her sandwich, and sliding down from the stool wandered outdoors.

"I wish I knew who those men are," she thought. "Francine could tell me if she weren't so horrid."

Penny waited until the last possible minute before boarding the plane. As she stepped inside the cabin she was surprised to see that Francine had taken the chair beside Maxine Miller, very coolly moving Penny's belongings to the seat at the back of the airliner.

"Did you two decide to change places?" inquired the stewardess as Penny hesitated beside the empty chair.

"I didn't decide. It just seems to be an accomplished fact."

The stewardess went down the aisle and touched Francine's arm. "Usually the passengers keep their same seats throughout the journey," she said with a pleasant smile. "Would you mind?"

Francine did mind for she had cut her lunch short in the hope of obtaining the coveted chair, but she could not refuse to move. Frowning, she went back to her former place.

Actually, Penny was not particular where she sat. There was no practical advantage in being directly behind the two strangers, for their voices were seldom audible above the roar of the plane. On the other hand, Miss Miller talked loudly and with scarcely a halt for breath. Penny was rather relieved when an early stop for dinner enabled her to gain a slight respite.

With flying conditions still favorable, the second half of the journey was begun. Penny curled up in her clean, comfortable bed, and the gentle rocking of the plane soon lulled her to sleep. She did not awaken until morning when the stewardess came to warn her they soon would be at their destination. Penny dressed speedily, and enjoyed a delicious breakfast brought to her on a tray. She had just finished when Francine staggered down the aisle, eyes bloodshot, her straight black hair looking as if it had never been combed.

"Will I be glad to get off this plane!" she moaned. "What a night!"

"I didn't notice anything wrong with it," said Penny. "I take it you didn't sleep well."

"Sleep? I never closed my eyes all night, not with this roller-coaster sliding down one mountain and up another. I thought every minute we were going to crash."

Maxine Miller likewise seemed to have spent an uncomfortable night, for her face was haggard and worn. She looked five years older and her make-up was smeared.

"Tell me, do I look too dreadful?" she asked Penny anxiously. "I want to appear my best when I meet Mr. Balantine."

"You'll have time to rest up before you see him," the girl replied kindly.

"How long before we reach Pine Top?"

"We should be approaching there now." Penny studied the terrain below with deep interest, noting mountain ranges and beautiful snowy valleys.

At last the plane circled and swept down on a small landing field which had been cleared of snow. Passengers began to pour from the cabin, grateful that the long journey was finally at an end.

"I hope I see you again," said Penny, extending her hand to Miss Miller. "And the best of luck with Mr. Balantine."

Eagerly, she gathered together her possessions and stepped out of the plane into blinding sunlight. The air was crisp and cold, but there was a quality to it which made her take long, deep breaths. Beyond the landing field stood a tall row of pine trees, each topped with a layer of snow like the white icing of a cake. From somewhere far away she could hear the merry jingle of sleigh bells.

"So this is Pine Top!" thought Penny. "It's as pretty as a Christmas card!"

A small group of persons were at the field to meet the plane. Catching sight of a short, sober-looking little woman who was bundled in furs, Penny hastened toward her.

"Mrs. Downey!" she cried.

"Penny, my dear! How glad I am to see you!" The woman clasped her firmly, planting a kiss on either cheek. "But your father shouldn't have disappointed me. Why didn't he come along?"

"He wanted to, but he's up to his eyebrows in trouble. A man is suing him for libel."

"Oh, that *is* bad," murmured Mrs. Downey. "I know what legal trouble means because I've had an unpleasant taste of it myself lately. But come, let's get your luggage and be starting up the mountain."

"Just a minute," said Penny in a low tone. With a slight inclination of her head, she indicated the two male passengers who had made the long journey from Riverview to Pine Top. "You don't by any chance know either of those men?"

Mrs. Downey's face lost its kindliness and she said, in a grim voice: "I certainly do!"

Before Penny could urge the woman to reveal their identity, Francine walked over to where she and Mrs. Downey stood.

"Did you wish to see me?" inquired the hotel woman as Francine looked at her with an inquiring gaze.

"Are you Mrs. Downey?"

"Yes, I am."

"I am looking for a place to stay," said Francine. "I was told that you keep an inn."

"Yes, we have a very nice lodge up the mountain about a mile from here. The rooms are comfortable, and I do most of the cooking myself. We're located on the best ski slopes in the valley. But if you're looking for a place with plenty of style and corresponding prices you might prefer the Fergus place."

"Your lodge will exactly suit me, I think," declared Francine. "How do I get there?"

"In my bob-sled," offered Mrs. Downey. "I may have a few other guests."

"It won't take me a minute to get my luggage," said Francine, moving away.

Penny was none too pleased to know that the girl reporter would make her headquarters at the Downey Inn. Her face must have mirrored her misgiving, for Mrs. Downey said apologetically:

"Business hasn't been any too good this season. I have to pick up an extra tourist whenever I can."

"Of course," agreed Penny hastily. "One can't run a hotel without guests."

"I do believe Jake has snared another victim," Mrs. Downey laughed. "That woman with the bleached hair."

"And who is Jake?" inquired Penny.

Mrs. Downey nodded her head toward a spry man with leathery skin who was talking with Maxine Miller.

"He does odd jobs for me at the Inn," she explained. "When he has no other occupation he tries to entice guests into our den."

"You make it sound like a very wicked business," chuckled Penny.

"Since the Fergus hotel was built it's become a struggle, to the death," replied Mrs. Downey soberly. "I truly believe this will be my last year at Pine Top."

"Why, you've had your home here for years," said Penny in astonishment. "You were at Pine Top long before anyone thought of it as a great skiing resort. You're an institution here, Mrs. Downey. Surely you aren't serious about giving up your lodge?"

"Yes, I am, Penny. But I shouldn't start telling my troubles the moment you arrive. I never would have said a word if you hadn't asked me about those two men yonder."

She gazed scornfully toward the strangers whose identity Penny hoped to learn.

"Who *are* they?" Penny asked quickly.

"The slim fellow with the sharp face is Ralph Fergus," answered Mrs. Downey, her voice filled with bitterness. "He manages the hotel and is supposed to be the owner. Actually, the other man is the one who provides all the money."

"And who is he?"

"Why, you should know," replied Mrs. Downey. "He has a hotel in Riverview. His name is Harvey Maxwell. He only comes here now and then."

"Harvey Maxwell!" repeated Penny. "Wait until Dad hears about this!"

"Your father has had dealings with him?"

"Has he?" murmured Penny. "Maxwell is the man who is suing Dad for libel!"

"Well, of all things!"

"I believe I understand why Francine came out here too," Penny said thoughtfully.

"Francine?"

"The girl who just engaged a room at your place. I think she went to your Inn for the sole purpose of keeping an eye on me."

"Why should she wish to do that?"

"Francine is a reporter for the *Riverview Record*. Dad's story about Maxwell bribing a football player served as a tip-off to other editors. Now the *Record* may hope to get evidence against him which they can build up into a big story."

"I should think that would help your father's case."

"It might," agreed Penny, "all depending upon how the evidence was used. But somehow, I don't trust Francine. If there's any fancy newspaper work to be done at Pine Top, I aim to look after it myself!"

***

CHAPTER 5

OVER THE BARBED WIRE

Mrs. Downey laughed at Penny's remark, not taking it very seriously. "I wish someone could uncover damaging evidence against Harvey Maxwell," she declared. "But I fear he's far too clever a man to be caught in anything dishonest. Sometime when you're in the mood to hear a tale of woe, I'll tell you how he is running things at Pine Top."

"I'd like to learn everything I can about him," responded Penny eagerly.

Mrs. Downey led the girl across the field to the road where the bob-sled and team of horses had been hitched. Jake, the handy man, appeared a moment later, loaded down with skis and luggage. Maxine Miller, Francine, and a well-dressed business man soon arrived and were helped into the sled.

"This is unique taxi service to say the least," declared Francine, none too well pleased. "It must take ages to get up the mountain."

"Not very long," replied Mrs. Downey cheerfully.

Jake drove, with the hotel woman and her guests sitting on the floor of the sled, covered by warm blankets.

"Is it always so cold here?" shivered Miss Miller.

"Always at this time of year," returned Mrs. Downey. "You'll not mind it in a day or two. And the skiing is wonderful. We had six more inches of snow last night."

Penny thoroughly enjoyed the novel experience of gliding swiftly over the hard-packed snow. The bobsled presently passed a large rustic building at the base of the mountain which Mrs. Downey pointed out as the Fergus hotel.

"I suppose all the rich people stay there," commented Miss Miller. "Do you know if they have a guest named David Balantine?"

"The producer? Yes, I believe he is staying at the Fergus hotel."

At the next bend Jake stopped the horses so that the girls might obtain a view of the valley.

"Over to the right is the village of Pine Top," indicated Mrs. Downey. "Just beyond the Fergus hotel is the site of an old silver mine, abandoned many years ago. And when we reach the next curve you'll be able to look north and see into Canada."

A short ride on up the mountain brought the party to the Downey Lodge, a small but comfortable log building amid the pines. On the summit of a slope not far away they could see the figure of a skier, poised for a swift, downward flight.

Mrs. Downey assigned the guests to their rooms, tactfully establishing Penny and Francine at opposite ends of a long hall.

"Luncheon will be served at one o'clock," she told them. "If you feel equal to it you'll have time for a bit of skiing."

"I believe I'll walk down to the village and send a wire to Dad," said Penny. "Then this afternoon I'll try my luck on the slopes."

"Just follow the road and you'll not get lost," instructed Mrs. Downey.

Penny unpacked her suitcase, and then set forth at a brisk walk for the village. She found the telegraph station without difficulty and dispatched a message to her father, telling him of Harvey Maxwell's presence in Pine Top.

The town itself, consisting of half a dozen stores and twice as many houses, was soon explored. Before starting back up the mountain Penny thought she would buy a morning newspaper. But as she made inquiry at a drug store, the owner shook his head.

"We don't carry them here. The only papers we get come in by plane. They're all sold out long before this."

"Oh, I see," said Penny in disappointment, "well, next time I'll try to come earlier."

"I beg your pardon," ventured a voice directly behind her. "Allow me to offer you my paper."

Penny turned around to see that Ralph Fergus had entered the drugstore in time to hear her remark. With a most engaging smile, he extended his own newspaper.

"Oh, I don't like to take your paper," she protested, wishing to accept no favor however small from the man.

"Please do," he urged, thrusting it into her hand. "I have finished with it."

"Thank you," said Penny.

She took the paper and started to leave the store. Mr. Fergus fell into step with her, following her outside.

"Going back up the mountain?" he inquired casually.

"Yes, I was."

"I'll walk along if you don't mind having company."

"Not at all."

Penny studied Ralph Fergus curiously, fairly certain he had a special reason for wishing to walk with her. For a time they trudged along in silence, the snow creaking beneath their boots.

"Staying at the Downey Lodge?" Fergus inquired after awhile.

"Yes, I am."

"Like it there?"

"Well, I only arrived on the morning plane."

"Yes, I noticed you aboard," he nodded. "Mrs. Downey is a very fine woman, a very fine woman, but her lodge isn't modern. You noticed that, I suppose?"

"I'm not especially critical," smiled Penny. "It seemed to suit my needs."

"You'll be more critical after you have stayed there a few days," he warned. "The service is very poor. Even this little matter of getting a morning newspaper. Now our hotel sees that every guest has one shoved under his door before breakfast."

"That would be very nice, I'm sure," remarked Penny dryly. "You're the manager of the hotel, aren't you?"

Ralph Fergus gave her a quick, appraising glance. "Right you are," he said jovially. "Naturally I think we have the finest hotel at Pine Top and I wish you would try it. I'll be glad to make you a special rate."

"You're very kind." It was a struggle for Penny to keep her voice casual. "I may drop around sometime and look the hotel over."

"Do that," he urged. "Here is my card. Just ask for me and I'll show you about."

Penny took the card and dropped it into her pocket. A few minutes later as they passed the Fergus hotel, her companion parted company with her.

"He thought I was an ordinary guest at Mrs. Downey's," Penny told herself. "Otherwise, he never would have dared to make such an open bid for my patronage."

Upon returning to the lodge she told Mrs. Downey of her meeting with Ralph Fergus.

"It doesn't surprise me one bit," the woman replied angrily. "Fergus has been using every method he can think of to get my guests away from me. He has runners out all the time, talking up his hotel and talking mine down."

Penny sat on the edge of the kitchen table, watching Mrs. Downey stir a great kettle of steaming soup.

"While I was coming here on the plane I heard Fergus and Maxwell speaking about you."

"You did, Penny? What did they have to say? Nothing good, I'll warrant."

"I couldn't understand what they meant at the time, but now I think I do. They said that nothing stood in their way except your place. Maxwell declared he would soon take care of you, and that he was on his way to Pine Top to show Fergus how such affairs were handled."

Mrs. Downey kept on stirring with the big spoon. "So the screws are to be twisted a bit harder?" she asked grimly.

"Why do they want your place?" Penny inquired.

"Because I take a few of their guests away from them. If my lodge closed up they could raise prices sky high, and they would do it, too!"

"They offered me a special rate, whatever that means."

"Fergus has been cutting his room rents lately for the sole purpose of getting my customers away from me. He makes up for it by charging three and even four dollars a meal. The guests don't learn that until after they have moved in."

"And there's nothing you can do about it?"

Mrs. Downey shook her head. "I've been fighting with my back to the wall this past season. I don't see how I possibly can make it another year. That is why I wanted you and your father to visit here before I gave up the place."

"Dad might have helped you," Penny said regretfully. "I'm sorry he wasn't able to come."

At one o'clock Mrs. Downey served a plain but substantial meal to fourteen guests who tramped in out of the snow. They called loudly for second and third helpings which were cheerfully given.

After luncheon Penny sat for a time about the crackling log fire and then she went to her room and changed into her skiing clothes.

"The nursery slopes are at the rear of the lodge," Mrs. Downey told her as she went out through the kitchen. "But you're much too experienced for them."

"I haven't been on skis for nearly two years."

"It will come back to you quickly."

"I thought I might taxi down and look over the Fergus hotel."

"The trail is well marked. Just be careful as you get about half way down. There is a sharp turn and if you miss it you may find yourself wrapped around an evergreen."

Penny went outside, and buckling on her skis, glided to the top of a long slope which fell rather sharply through lanes of pine trees to the wide valley below. As she was studying the course, reflecting that the crusted snow would be very fast, Francine came out of the lodge and stood watching her.

"What's the matter, Penny?" she called. "Can't you get up your nerve?"

Penny dug in her poles and pushed off. Crouching low, skis running parallel, she tore down the track. Pine trees crowded past on either side in a greenish blur. The wind whistled in her ears. She jabbed her poles into the snow to check her speed.

After the first steep stretch, the course flattened out slightly. From a cautious left traverse, a lifted stem turn gave her time to concentrate her full attention on the route ahead. She swerved to avoid a boulder which would have broken her ski had she crashed into it, and rode out a series of long, undulating hollows.

Gathering speed again, Penny made her decisions with lightning rapidity. There was no time to think. Confronted with a choice of turns, she chose the right hand trail, slashing through in a beautiful christiana. Too late, she realized her error.

Directly ahead loomed a barbed wire fence. There was no opportunity to turn aside. Penny knew that she must jump or take a disastrous fall.

Swinging her poles forward, she let them drop in the snow close to her ski tips. Crouching low she sprang upward with all her strength. The sticks gave her leverage so that she could lift her skis clear of the snow. Momentum carried her forward over the fence.

Penny felt the jar of the runners as they slapped on the snow. Then she lost her balance and tumbled head over heels.

Untangling herself, she sat up and gazed back at the barbed wire fence.

"I wish all my friends at Riverview could have seen that jump!" she thought proudly. "It was a beauty even if I did land wrong side up."

A large painted sign which had been fastened to the fence, drew her attention. It read: "Skiers Keep Out."

"I wonder if that means me?" remarked Penny aloud.

"Yes, it means you!" said an angry voice behind her.

Penny rolled over in the snow, waving her skis in the air. She drew in her breath sharply. An old man with a dark beard had stepped from the shadow of the pine trees, a gun grasped in his gnarled hands!

***

CHAPTER 6

PENNY TRESPASSES

"Can't you understand signs?" the old man demanded, advancing with cat-like tread from the fringe of pine trees.

"Not when I'm traveling down a mountain side at two hundred miles an hour!" Penny replied. "Please, would you mind pointing that cannon in some other direction? It might go off."

The old man lowered the shotgun, but the grim lines of his wrinkled, leathery face did not relax.

"Get up!" he commanded, prodding her with the toe of his heavy boot. "Get out of here! I won't have you or any other skier on my property."

"Then allow me to make a suggestion," remarked Penny pleasantly. "Put up another strand of barbed wire and you'll have them all in the hospital!"

She sat up, gingerly felt of her left ankle and then began to brush snow from her jacket. "Did you see me make the jump?" she asked. "I took it just like a reindeer. Or do I mean a gazelle?"

"You made a very awkward jump!" he retorted. "I could have done better myself."

Penny glanced up with genuine interest. "Oh, do you ski?"

By this time she no longer was afraid of the old man, if indeed she had ever been.

"No, I don't ski!" he answered impatiently. "Now hurry up! Get those skis off and start moving! I'll not wait all day."

Penny began to unstrap the long hickory runners, but with no undue show of haste. She glanced curiously about the snowy field. An old shed stood not far away. Beside it towered a great stack of wood which reached nearly as high as the roof. Through the trees she caught a glimpse of a weather-stained log cabin with smoke curling lazily from the brick chimney.

As Penny was regarding it, she saw a flash of color at one of the windows. A girl who might have been her own age had her face pressed against the pane. Seeing Penny's gaze upon her, she began to make motions which could not be understood.

The old man also turned his head to look toward the cabin. Immediately, the girl disappeared from the window.

"Is that where you live?" inquired Penny.

Instead of answering, the old man seized her by the hand and pulled her to her feet.

"Go!" he commanded. "And don't let me catch you here again!"

Penny shouldered her skis and moved toward the fence.

"So sorry to have damaged your nice snow," she apologized. "I'll try not to trespass again."

Crawling under the barbed wire fence, Penny retraced her way up the slope to the point on the trail where she had taken the wrong turn. There she hesitated and finally decided to walk on to the Fergus hotel.

"I wonder who that girl was at the window?" Penny reflected as she trudged along. "She looked too young to be Old Whisker's daughter. And what was she trying to tell me?"

The problem was too deep for her to solve. But she made up her mind she would ask Mrs. Downey the name of the queer old man as soon as she returned to the lodge.

Reaching the Fergus hotel, Penny parked her skis upright in a snowbank near the front door, and went inside. She found herself in a long lobby at the end of which was a great stone fireplace with a half burned log on the hearth. Bellboys in green uniforms and brass buttons darted to and fro. A general stir of activity pervaded the place.

As Penny was gazing about, she saw Maxine Miller leave an elevator and come slowly across the lobby. The actress would not have seen her had she not spoken.

"How do you do, Miss Miller. I didn't expect to see you here."

"Oh, Miss Parker!" The actress' face was the picture of despair. "I've had the most wretched misfortune!"

"Why, what has happened?" inquired Penny, although she thought she knew the answer to her question.

"I've just seen Mr. Balantine." Miss Miller sagged into the depths of a luxuriously upholstered davenport and leaned her head back against the cushion.

"Your interview didn't turn out as you expected?"

"He wouldn't give me the part. Hateful old goat! He even refused to allow me to demonstrate how well I could read the lines! And he said some very insulting things to me."

"That is too bad," returned Penny sympathetically. "What will you do now? Go back home?"

"I don't know," the woman replied in despair. "I would stay if I thought I could change Mr. Balantine's opinion. Do you think I could?"

"I shouldn't advise it myself. Of course, I don't know anything about Mr. Balantine."

"He's very temperamental. Perhaps if I kept bothering him he would finally give me a chance."

"Well, it might be worth trying," Penny said doubtfully. "But I think if I were you I would return home."

"All of my friends will laugh at me. They thought it was foolish to come out here as it was. I can't go back. I am inclined to move down to this hotel so I'll be able to keep in touch with Mr. Balantine with less difficulty."

"It's a very nice looking hotel," commented Penny. "Expensive, I've been told."

"In the show business one must keep up appearances at all cost," replied Miss Miller. "I believe I'll inquire about the rates."

While Penny waited, the actress crossed over to the desk and talked with a clerk. In a small office close by, Ralph Fergus and Harvey Maxwell could be seen in consultation. They were poring over a ledger, apparently checking business accounts.

Miss Miller returned in a moment. "I've taken a room," she announced. "I can't afford it, but I am doing it anyway."

"Will you be able to manage?"

"Oh, I'll run up a bill and then let them try to collect!"

Penny gazed at the actress with frank amazement.

"You surely don't mean you would deliberately defraud the hotel?"

"Not so loud or the clerk will hear you," Miss Miller warned. "And don't use such an ugly word. If I land the part with Mr. Balantine, of course I'll pay. If not—the worst they can do is to throw me out."

Penny said no more but her opinion of Miss Miller had descended several notches.

"What are you doing here?" the actress inquired, quickly changing the subject.

"Oh, I just came down to look over the hotel. It's very swanky, but I like Mrs. Downey's place better."

Miss Miller turned to leave. "I am going back there now to check out," she declared. "Would you like to walk along?"

"No, thank you, I'll just stay here and rest for a few minutes."

Penny had no real purpose in coming to the Fergus hotel. She merely had been curious to see what it was like. Even a casual inspection made it clear that Mrs. Downey's modest little lodge never could compete with such a luxurious establishment.

She studied the faces of the persons in the lobby. There seemed to be a strange assortment of people, including a large number of men and women who certainly had never been drawn to Pine Top by the skiing. Penny thought whimsically that it would be interesting to see some of the fat, pampered-looking ones take a tumble on the slippery slopes.

"But what is the attraction of this place, if not the skiing?" she puzzled. "There is no other form of entertainment."

Presently, a well-fed lady in rustling black silk, her hand heavy with diamond rings, paused beside Penny.

"I beg your pardon," she said, "can you tell me how to find the Green Room?"

"No, I can't," replied Penny. "I would need a map to get around in this hotel. You might ask at the desk."

The woman fluttered over to the clerk and asked the same question.

"You have your card, Madam?" he inquired in a low tone.

"Oh, yes, to be sure. The manager presented it to me this morning."

"Take the elevator to the second floor wing," the man instructed. "Room 22. Show your card to the doorman and you will be admitted."

Penny waited until after the woman had gone away. Then she arose and sauntered across the lobby. She picked up a handful of hotel literature but there was no mention of any Green Room. Pausing by the elevator, she waited until the cage was deserted of passengers before speaking to the attendant, a red headed boy of about seventeen.

"Where is the Green Room, please?"

"Second floor, Miss."

"And what is it? A dining room?"

The attendant shot her a peculiar glance and gave an answer which was equally strange.

"It's not a dining room. I can't tell you what it is."

"A cocktail room perhaps?"

"Listen, I told you I don't know," the boy answered.

"You work here, don't you?"

"Sure I do," he said with emphasis. "And I aim to keep my job for awhile. If you want to know anything about the Green Room ask at the desk!"

***

CHAPTER 7

THE GREEN DOOR

Before Penny could ask another question, the signal board flashed a summons, and the attendant slammed shut the door of the elevator. He shot the cage up to the fifth floor and did not return.

Hesitating a moment, Penny wandered over to the desk.

"How does one go about obtaining a card for the Green Room?" she inquired casually.

"You're not a guest here?" questioned the clerk.

"No."

"You'll have to talk with the manager. Oh, Mr. Fergus!"

Penny had not meant to have the matter go so far, but there was no retreating. The hotel manager came out of his office, and recognizing her, smiled ingratiatingly.

"Ah, good afternoon, Miss—" He groped for her name but Penny did not supply it. "So you decided to pay us a visit after all."

"This young lady asked about the Green Room," said the clerk significantly.

Mr. Fergus bestowed a shrewd, appraising look upon Penny.

"Oh, yes," he said to give himself more time, "Oh, yes, I see. What was it you wished to know?"

"How does one obtain a card of admission?"

"It is very simple. That is, if you have the proper recommendations and bank credit."

"Recommendations?" Penny asked blankly. "Just what is the Green Room anyway?"

Ralph Fergus and the clerk exchanged a quick glance which was not lost upon the girl.

"I see you are not familiar with the little service which is offered hotel guests," Mr. Fergus said suavely. "I shall be most happy to explain it to you at some later time when I am not quite so busy."

He bowed and went hurriedly back into the office.

"I guess I shouldn't have inquired about the Green Room," Penny observed aloud. "There seems to be a deep mystery connected with it."

"No mystery," corrected the clerk. "If you will leave your name and address I am sure everything can be arranged within a few days."

"Thank you, I don't believe I'll bother."

Penny turned and nearly ran into Francine Sellberg. Too late, she realized that the girl reporter probably had been standing by the desk for some time, listening to her conversation.

"Hello, Francine," she said carelessly.

The girl returned a haughty stare. "I don't believe I know you, Miss," she said, and walked on across the lobby.

Penny was rather stunned by the unexpected snub. She took a step as if to follow Francine and demand an explanation, but her sense of humor came to her rescue.

"Who cares?" she asked herself with a shrug. "If she doesn't care to know me, it's perfectly all right. I can manage to bear up."

After Francine had left the hotel, Penny made up her mind that she would try to learn a little more about the Green Room. Her interest was steadily mounting and she could not imagine what "service" might be offered guests in this particular part of the hotel.

Choosing a moment when no one appeared to be watching, Penny mounted the stairway to the second floor. She followed a long corridor to its end but did not locate Room 22. Returning to the elevator, she started in the opposite direction. The numbers ended at 20.

While Penny was trying to figure it out, a group of four men and women came down the hall. They were well dressed individuals but their manner did not stamp them as persons of good breeding. One of the women who carried a jeweled handbag was talking in a loud, excited tone:

"Oh, Herbert, wait until you see it! I shall weep my eyes out if you don't agree to buy it for me at once. And the price! Ridiculously cheap! We'll never run into bargains like these in New York."

"We'll see, Sally," replied the man. "I'm not satisfied yet that this isn't a flim-flam game."

He opened a door which bore no number, and stood aside for the others to pass ahead of him. Penny caught a glimpse of a long, empty hallway.

"That must be the way to Room 22," she thought.

She waited until the men and women had gone ahead, and then cautiously opened the door which had closed behind them. No one questioned her as she moved noiselessly down the corridor. At its very end loomed a green painted door, its top edge gracefully circular. Beside it at a small table sat a man who evidently was stationed there as a guard.

Penny walked slowly, watching the men and women ahead. They paused at the table and showed slips of cardboards. The guard then opened the green door and allowed them to pass through.

It looked so very easy that Penny decided to try her luck. She drew closer.

"Your card please," requested the doorman.

"I am afraid I haven't mine with me," said Penny, flashing her most beguiling smile.

The smile was entirely lost upon the man. "Then I can't let you in," he said.

"Not even if I have lost my card?"

"Orders," he answered briefly. "You'll have no trouble getting another."

Penny started to turn away, and then asked with attempted carelessness:

"What's going on in there anyway? Are they selling something?"

"I really couldn't tell you," he responded.

"Everyone in this hotel seems to be blind, deaf and dumb," Penny muttered to herself as she retraced her way to the main hall. "And definitely, for a purpose. I wonder if maybe I haven't stumbled into something?"

She still had not the faintest idea what might lie beyond the Green Door, but the very name had an intriguing sound. It suggested mystery. It suggested, too, that Ralph Fergus and his financial backer, Harvey Maxwell, might have developed some special money-making scheme which would not bear exposure.

Into Penny's mind leaped a remark which her father had made, one to the effect that Harvey Maxwell was thought to have his finger in many dishonest affairs. The Green Room might be a perfectly legitimate place of entertainment for hotel guests, but the remarks she had overheard led Penny to think otherwise. Something was being sold in Room 22. And to a very select clientele!

"If only I could learn facts which would help Dad's case!" she told herself. "Anything showing that Maxwell is mixed up in a dishonest scheme might turn the trick!"

It occurred to Penny that the editor of the *Riverview Record* might have had some inkling of a story to be found at Pine Top. Otherwise, why had Francine been sent to the mountain resort? Certainly the rival reporter was working upon an assignment which concerned Harvey Maxwell. She inadvertently had revealed that fact at the Riverview airport.

"Francine thinks I came here for the same purpose," mused Penny. "If only she weren't so high-hat we could work together."

There was almost no real evidence to point to a conclusion that the Fergus hotel was not being operated properly. Penny realized only too well that once more she was depending upon a certain intuition. An investigation of the Green Room might reveal no mystery. But at least there was a slender hope she could learn something which would aid her father in discrediting Harvey Maxwell.

Without attracting attention, Penny descended to the main floor and left the hotel. As she retrieved her skis from the snowbank she was surprised to see Francine standing close by, obviously waiting for her.

"Hello, Penny," the girl greeted her.

"Goodness! Aren't you mistaken? I don't think you know me!"

"Oh, don't try to be funny," Francine replied, falling into step. "I'll explain."

"I wish you would."

"You should have known better than to shout out my name there in the lobby."

"I don't follow your reasoning at all, Francine. Are you traveling incognito or something?"

"Naturally I don't care to have it advertised that I am a reporter. I rather imagine you're not overly anxious to have it known that you are the daughter of Anthony Parker either!"

"It probably wouldn't be any particular help," admitted Penny.

"Exactly! Despite your play-acting at the airport, I know you came here to get the low-down on Harvey Maxwell. But the minute he learns who you are you'll not even get inside the hotel."

"And that goes double, I take it?"

"No one at Pine Top except you knows I am a reporter," went on Francine without answering. "So I warn you, don't pull another boner like you did a few minutes ago. Whenever we're around Fergus or Maxwell or persons who might report to them, just remember you never saw me before. Is that clear?"

"Moderately so," drawled Penny.

"I guess that's all I have to say." Francine hesitated and started to walk off.

"Wait a minute, Francine," spoke Penny impulsively. "Why don't we bury the hatchet and work together on this thing? After all I am more interested in gaining evidence against Maxwell than I am in getting a big story for the paper. How about it?"

Francine smiled in a superior way.

"Thank you, I prefer to lone wolf it. You see, I happen to have a very good lead, and you don't."

"Well, I've heard about the Green Room," said Penny, hazarding a shot in the dark. "That's something."

Francine stopped short.

"What do you know about it?" she demanded quickly. "Maybe we could work together after all."

Penny laughed as she bent down to strap on her skis.

"No, thanks," she declined pleasantly. "You once suggested that a clever reporter finds his own answers. You'll have to wait until you read it in the *Star*!"

***

CHAPTER 8

A CODED MESSAGE

Penny sat in the kitchen of Mrs. Downey's lodge, warming her half frozen toes in the oven.

"Well, how did you like the skiing?" inquired her hostess who was busy mixing a huge meat loaf to be served for dinner.

"It was glorious," answered Penny, "only I took a bad spill. Somehow I missed the turn you told me about, and found myself heading for a barbed wire fence. I jumped it and made a one point landing in a snowbank!"

"You didn't hurt yourself, thank goodness."

"No, but an old man with a shotgun came out of the woods and said 'Scat!' to me. It seems he doesn't like skiers."

"That must have been Peter Jasko."

"And who is he, Mrs. Downey?"

"One of the oldest settlers on Pine Top Mountain," sighed Mrs. Downey. "He's a very pleasant man in some respects, but in others—oh, dear."

"Skiing must be one of his unpleasant aspects. I noticed he had a 'Keep Out' sign posted on his property."

"Peter Jasko is a great trial to me and other persons on the mountain. He has a hatred of skiing and everything pertaining to it, which amounts to fanaticism. A number of skiers have been injured by running into his barbed wire fence."

"Then he put it up on purpose?"

"Oh, yes! He has an idea it will keep folks from skiing."

"He isn't—?" Penny tapped her forehead significantly.

"No," smiled Mrs. Downey. "Old Peter is right in his mind, at least in every respect save this one. He owns our best ski slopes, too."

Penny shifted her foot to a cooler place in the oven.

"Not the slopes connected with this lodge?"

Mrs. Downey nodded as she whipped eggs to a foamy yellow.

"I leased the land from Jasko's son many years ago, and Jasko can do nothing about it except rage. However, the lease expires soon. He has given me to understand it will not be renewed."

"Can't you deal with the son?"

"He is dead, Penny."

"Oh, I see. That does make it difficult."

"Decidedly. Jasko's attitude about the lease is another reason why I think this will be my last year in the hotel business."

"You don't think Ralph Fergus or Harvey Maxwell have influenced Jasko?" Penny asked thoughtfully, a frown ridging her forehead.

"I doubt that anyone could influence the old man," replied Mrs. Downey. "Stubborn isn't the word to describe his character. Even if I lose the ski slopes, I am quite sure he will never lease them to the Fergus hotel interests."

"While I was down there I thought I saw a girl standing at the window of the cabin."

"Probably you did, Penny. Jasko has a granddaughter about your age, named Sara. A very nice girl, too, but she is kept close at home."

"I feel sorry for her if she has to live with that old man. He seemed like a regular ogre."

Removing her toasted feet from the oven, Penny pulled on her stiff boots again. Without bothering to lace them, she hobbled toward the door.

                                                        Behind the Green Door

"Oh, by the way," she remarked, pausing. "Did you ever hear of a Green Room at the Fergus hotel?"

"A Green Room?" repeated Mrs. Downey. "No, I can't say I have. What is it, Penny?"

"I wonder myself. Something funny seems to be going on there."

Having aroused Mrs. Downey's curiosity, Penny gave a more complete account of her visit to the Fergus hotel.

"I've never heard anyone mention such a place," declared the woman in a puzzled voice. "But I will say this. The hotel always has attracted a peculiar group of guests."

"How would you like to have me solve the mystery for you?" joked Penny.

"It would suit me very well indeed," laughed Mrs. Downey. "And while you're about it you might put Ralph Fergus out of business, and bring me a new flock of guests."

"I'm afraid you're losing one instead. Maxine Miller told me she is moving down to the big hotel."

"I know. She checked out a half hour ago. Jake made an extra trip to haul her luggage down the mountain."

"Anyway, I shouldn't be sorry to see her go if I were you," comforted Penny. "I am quite sure she hasn't enough money to pay for a week's stay at Pine Top."

Going to her room, Penny changed into more comfortable clothing and busied herself writing a long letter to her father. From her desk by the window she could see skiers trudging up the slopes, some of them making neat herring-bone tracks, others slipping and sliding, losing almost as much distance as they gained.

As she watched, Francine swung into view, poling rhythmically, in perfect timing with her long easy strides.

"She *is* good," thought Penny, grudgingly.

Dinner was served at six. Afterwards, the guests sat before the crackling log fire and bored each other with tales of their skiing prowess.

A few of the more enterprising ones waxed their skis in preparation for the next day's sport.

"Any newspapers tonight?" inquired a business man of Mrs. Downey. "Or is this another one of the blank days?"

"Jake brought New York papers from the village," replied the hotel woman. "They are on the table."

"Blank days?" questioned Francine, looking up from a magazine she had been reading.

"Mr. Glasser calls them that when he doesn't get the daily stock market report," explained Mrs. Downey, smiling at her guest.

"And don't the newspapers always arrive?" questioned Francine.

"Not always. Lately the service has been very poor."

"I'd rather be deprived of a meal than my paper," growled Mr. Glasser. "What annoys me is that the guests at the Fergus hotel always get their papers. I wish someone would explain it to me."

"And I wish someone would explain it to *me*," murmured Mrs. Downey, retreating to the kitchen.

In the morning Penny decided to ski down to the village for a jar of cold cream. The snow was crusted and fast but she felt no terror of the trail which curved sharply through the evergreens. Her balance was better, and this time she had no intention of impaling herself on Peter Jasko's barbed wire fence.

Seldom checking her speed, she hurtled along the ribbon of trail. Racing on to the sharp turn, she shifted her weight and swung her body at precisely the right instant. The slope stretched on past rows of tall trees, towering like sentinels along the snow-swept ridges. Presently it flattened out into an open valley. Penny sailed past a house, a barn, and gradually slowed up until she came to a low hillock overlooking the village.

Recapturing her breath, Penny took off her skis and walked on into Pine Top. She made a few purchases at the drug store and then impulsively entered the telegraph office. To her surprise, Francine Sellberg was there ahead of her.

"How late is your office open?" the reporter was asking the operator.

"Six-thirty," he replied.

"And if one has a rush message to send after that hour?"

"Well, you can get me at my house," the man answered. "I live over behind the Albert's Filling Station."

"Thank you," responded Francine, flashing Penny a mocking smile. "I may have an important story to send to my paper any hour. I wanted to be sure there would be no delay in getting it off."

Penny waited until the reporter had left the office and then said apologetically:

"I don't suppose you've received any message for me?"

"We always telephone as soon as anything comes in," the man replied. "But wait! You're Penelope Parker, aren't you?"

"In my more serious moments. Otherwise, just plain Penny."

"I do have something for you, then. A message came in a few minutes ago. I've been too busy to telephone it to the lodge."

He handed Penny a sheet of paper which she read eagerly. As she anticipated, it was from her father, and with his usual disregard for economy he had not bothered to omit words.

"Glad to learn you arrived safely at Pine Top," he had wired. "Your information about H. M. is astonishing, if true. Are you sure it is the same man? Keep your eye on him, and report to me if you learn anything worth while. I am held here by important developments, but will try to come to Pine Top for Christmas."

Penny read the message twice, scowling at the sentence: "Are you sure it is the same man?" It was clear to her that her father did not have a great deal of faith in her identification. And obviously, he did not believe that anything could be gained by making a special trip to Pine Top to see the hotel man.

Thrusting the paper into the pocket of her jacket she went out into the cold.

"No one seems to rate my detective work very highly," she complained to herself. "But when Dad gets my letter telling him about the Green Door he may take a different attitude!"

Skis slung over her shoulder, she began the weary climb back to the Downey lodge. Before Penny had walked very far she saw that she was overtaking a man on the narrow trail ahead of her. Observing that it was Ralph Fergus, she immediately slowed her steps.

The hotel man did not turn his head to glance back. He kept walking slower and slower as if in deep thought, and after a time he reached absently into his pocket for a letter.

As he pulled it out, another piece of pale gray paper fluttered to the ground. Fergus did not notice that he had lost anything. The wind caught the paper and blew it down the slope toward Penny.

"Oh, Mr. Fergus!" she called. "You dropped something!"

The wind hurled her words back at her. Realizing that she could not make the man hear, Penny quickened her pace. After a short chase she rescued the paper when it caught on the thorns of a snow-caked bush.

At first glance Penny thought she had gone to trouble for no purpose. The paper seemed to be blank. But as she turned it over she saw a single line of jumbled letters:

YL GFZKY GLULFFLS

"What can this be?" Penny thought in amazement. "Nothing, I guess."

She crumpled the paper and tossed it away. But as it skittered and bounced like a tumble weed down the trail, she suddenly changed her mind and darted after it again. Carefully straightening out the page she examined it a second time.

"This looks like copy paper used in a newspaper office," she told herself. "But there is no newspaper in Pine Top, I wonder—?"

The conviction came to Penny that the jumbled letters might be in code. Her pulse leaped at the thought. If only she were able to decipher it!

"I'll take this to the lodge and work on it," she decided quickly. "Who knows? It may be just the key I need to unlock this strange affair of the Green Door!"

***

CHAPTER 9

A CALL FOR HELP

All that afternoon and far into the evening Penny devoted to her assigned task, trying to make sense out of the jumbled sentence of typewriting. She used first one method and then another, but she could not decode the brief message. She had moments when she even doubted that it was a code. At last, completely disgusted, she threw down her pencil and put the paper away in a bureau drawer.

"I never was meant to be a cryptographer or whatever you call those brainy fellows who unravel ciphers and things!" she grumbled. "Maybe the trouble with me is that I'm not bright."

Switching off the lamp, Penny rolled up the shade, and stood for a moment gazing down into the dark valley. Far below she could see lights glowing in the Fergus hotel, mysterious and challenging.

"I feel as if I'm on the verge of an important discovery, yet nothing happens," she sighed. "Something unusual is going on here, but what?"

Penny did not believe that Francine knew the answer either. The girl reporter undoubtedly had been sent to Pine Top upon a definite tip from her editor, yet she could not guess the nature of such a tip. It was fairly evident that Francine was after some sort of evidence, but so far she had made no progress in acquiring it.

"We're both groping in the dark, searching for something we know is here but can't see," thought Penny. "And we watch each other like hawks for fear the other fellow will get the jump!"

The Green Door intrigued and puzzled her. While it might mean nothing at all, she could not shake off a feeling that if once she were able to get inside the room she might learn the answer to some of her questions.

Penny had turned over several plans in her mind, none of which suited her. The most obvious thing to do was to try to bribe an employee of the hotel to give her the information she sought. But if she failed, her identity would be disclosed to Ralph Fergus and Harvey Maxwell. It seemed wiser to bide her time and watch.

Penny awoke the next morning to find large flakes of snow piling on the window sills. The storm continued and after breakfast only the most rugged skiers ventured out on the slopes. Francine hugged a hot air register, complaining that there was not enough heat, Many of the other guests, soon exhausting the supply of magazines, became restless.

Luncheon was over when Penny stamped in out of the cold to find Mr. Glasser fretfully pacing to and fro before the fireplace.

"When will the papers come?" he asked Mrs. Downey.

"Jake usually goes down to the village after them about four o'clock. But with this thick weather, the plane may not get in today."

"It's in now, Mrs. Downey," spoke Penny, shaking snow from her red mittens. "I saw it nearly half an hour ago, flying low over the valley."

"Then the papers must be at Pine Top by this time." Mrs. Downey hesitated before adding: "I'll call Jake from his work and ask him to go after them."

"Let me," offered Penny quickly.

"In this storm?"

"Oh, I don't mind. I rather like it."

"All right, then," agreed Mrs. Downey in relief. "But don't get lost, whatever you do. If the trails become snowed over it might be better to stay on the main road."

"I won't get lost," laughed Penny. "If worse comes to worst I always can climb a pine tree and sight the Fergus hotel."

She dried out her mittens, and putting on an extra sweater beneath her jacket, stepped outside the lodge. The wind had fallen and only a few snowflakes were whirling down. Hearing the faint tingle of bells, Penny turned to gaze toward the road, where a pair of white horses were pulling an empty lumber wagon up the hill.

The driver, hunched over on the seat, was slapping his hands together to keep them warm.

"Why, that looks like Old Whiskers himself," thought Penny. "It is Peter Jasko."

The observation served only to remind her of their unpleasant meeting. Since being so discourteously ejected from the Jasko property Penny had not ventured back. Knowing that the old man was away she felt sorely tempted to again visit the locality.

"I guess I ought not to take the time," she decided regretfully. "Mr. Glasser will be fretting for his paper."

Making a quick trip down the mountainside, Penny swung into the village. Mrs. Downey had told her that she would be able to get the newspapers at the Pine Top Cafe where a boy named Benny Smith had an agency.

Entering the restaurant, she glanced about but saw no one who was selling papers. Finally, she ventured to ask the proprietor if she had come to the right place.

"This is the right place," he agreed cheerfully. "Benny went home a little while ago."

"Then how do I get the papers for Mrs. Downey's lodge?"

"Guess you're out of luck," he replied. "They didn't come in today."

"But I saw the plane."

"The plane got through all right. I don't know what was wrong. Somehow the papers weren't put aboard."

Penny turned away in disappointment. She had made the long trip to the village for no purpose. While she did not mind for herself, she knew that Mr. Glasser and the other guests were likely to be annoyed. After a day of confinement indoors they looked forward to news from the outside world.

"It's strange the papers didn't come," she mused as she started back to the Downey lodge. "This isn't the first time they've failed to arrive either."

Penny climbed steadily for a time and then sat down on a log to rest a moment. She was not far from the Jasko cabin. By making her own trail through the woods she could reach it in a very few minutes.

A mischievous idea leaped into her mind, fairly teasing to be put into effect. What fun to climb the forbidden barbed wire fence and honeycomb Mr. Jasko's field with ski tracks! She could visualize his annoyance when he returned home to learn that a mysterious skier had paid him a visit.

"He oughtn't to be so mean," she said aloud to justify herself. "It will serve him right for trying to frighten folks with shotguns!"

Penny fastened on her skis and glided off through the woods. She kept her directions straight and soon emerged into a clearing to find herself in view of the Jasko cabin. Drawing near the barbed wire fence she stopped short and stared.

"Why, that old scamp! He really did it!"

A new strand of wire had been added to the fence, making it many inches higher. Penny's suggestion, offered as a joke, had been acted upon by Peter Jasko. Not even an expert ski jumper could hope to clear the improved barrier. Any person who came unwittingly down the steep slope must take a disastrous tumble at the base of the fence.

"This settles it," thought Penny grimly. "My conscience is perfectly clear now."

She rolled under the fence and surveyed the unblemished expanse of snowy field with the eye of a mechanical draftsman.

"I may as well be honest about it and sign my name," she chuckled.

Starting in at the far corner of the field she made a huge double-edged "P" with her long runners. It took a little ingenuity to figure out an "E" but two "N's" were fairly easy to execute. She finished "Y" off with a flourish and cocked her head sideways to view her handiwork.

"Not bad, not bad at all," she congratulated herself. "Only I've used up too much space. We'll have to have a big Penny and a little Parker."

She ran off a "P" and an "A" but even her limber body was not equal to the contortion required for an "R." In the process of making a neat curve she suddenly lost her balance and toppled over in an ungainly heap.

"Oh, now I've done it!" she moaned, slowly picking herself up. "All my wonderful artistry gone for nothing. 'Parker' looks like a big smudge!"

A sound, suspiciously suggesting a muffled shout of laughter, reached Penny's ears. She glanced quickly about. No one was in sight. The windows of the cabin were deserted.

"I think I'll be getting out of here," she decided. "If Old Whiskers should come back this wouldn't be a healthy place to practice handwriting."

Penny dug in her poles and glided toward the fence. In the act of rolling under the barbed wires, she suddenly froze motionless. She had heard a cry and this time there was no doubt in her mind as to the direction from which the sound had come. Her startled gaze focused upon the cabin amid the trees.

"Help! Help!" called a shrill, half muffled voice. "Come back, and let me out of my prison!"

***

CHAPTER 10

LOCKED IN THE CABIN

Penny hesitated, and as the call was repeated, went slowly back toward the cabin. She could see no one.

"Up here!" shouted the voice.

Glancing toward the second story windows, Penny saw a girl standing there, her face pressed to the pane.

"Peter Jasko's granddaughter!" thought Penny. "And she must have seen me decorating the place with ski tracks."

However, the other girl was only concerned with her own predicament. She smiled and motioned for Penny to come directly under the window.

"Can you help me get out of here?" she called down.

"You're not locked in?" inquired Penny in astonishment.

"I certainly am! My grandfather did it. He fastened the door of the loft."

"How long have you been there?"

"Oh, not very long," the girl answered impatiently, "but I'm sick of it! Will you help me out of here?"

"How?"

"Grandfather always hides the key to the outside door in the woodshed. It should be hanging on a nail by the window."

Penny hardly knew what to do. It was one thing to annoy Peter Jasko by making a few ski tracks in his yard, but quite another to antagonize him in more serious ways. For all she could tell, he might have locked the girl in the cabin as a punishment for some wrongdoing.

"Does your grandfather often leave you like this?" she asked dubiously.

"Always when there's snow on the ground," came the surprising answer. "Oh, please let me out of this hateful place! Don't be such a goody-good!"

To be accused of being a "goody-good" was a novel experience for Penny. But instead of taking offense she laughed and started toward the woodshed.

"On a nail by the window!" the girl shouted after her. "If it isn't there look on the shelf by the door."

Penny found the key and came back. Taking off her cumbersome skis, she unlocked the front door and stepped inside the cabin. The room was rather cold for the fire had nearly gone out. Despite a bareness of furniture, the place had a comfortable appearance. Snowshoes decorated the walls along with a deer head and an out-dated calendar. There was a cook stove, a homemade table, chairs, and a cot.

"Do hurry up!" called the impatient voice from above. "Climb the steps."

At the far end of the room a rickety, crudely constructed ladder ascended to a rectangular trap door in the ceiling. Mounting it, Penny investigated the fastening, a stout plug of wood. She turned it and pushed up the heavy door. Instantly, it was seized from above and pulled out of the way.

Head and shoulders through the opening, Penny glanced about curiously. The room under the roof certainly did not look like a prison cell. It was snug and warm, with curtains at the windows and books lining the wall shelves. The floor was covered with a bright colored rag rug. There was a comfortable looking bed, a rocker and even a dressing table.

"Thanks for letting me out."

Penny turned to gaze at the girl who stood directly behind her. She was not very pretty, for her nose was far too blunt and her teeth a trifle uneven. One could see a faint resemblance to Peter Jasko.

"You're welcome, I guess," replied Penny, but with no conviction. "I hope your grandfather won't be too angry."

"Oh, he won't know about it," the girl answered carelessly. "I see you know who I am—Sara Jasko."

"My name is Penny Parker."

"I guessed the Penny part. I saw you trying to write it in the snow. You don't believe in signs either, do you?"

"I didn't have any right to trespass."

"Oh, don't worry about that. Grandfather is an old fuss-budget. But deep down inside he's rather nice."

"Why did he lock you up here?"

"It's a long story," sighed Sara. "I'll tell you about it later. Come on, let's get out of here."

Penny backed down the ladder. The amazing granddaughter of Peter Jasko followed, taking the steps as nimbly as a monkey.

Going to a closet, Sara pulled out a wind-breaker, woolen cap, and a stub-toed pair of high leather shoes which she began to lace up.

"You're not aiming to run away?" Penny asked uneasily.

"Only for an hour or so. This snow is too beautiful to waste. But you'll have to help me get back to my prison."

"I don't know what this is all about. Suppose you tell me, Sara."

"Oh, Grandfather is funny," replied the girl, digging in the closet again for her woolen gloves. "He doesn't trust me out of his sight when there's snow on the ground. Today he had to go up the mountain to get a load of wood so he locked me in."

"What has snow to do with it?"

"Why, everything! You must have heard about Grandfather. He hates skiing."

"Oh, and you like to ski," said Penny, "is that it?"

"I adore it! My father, Bret Jasko, was a champion." Sara's animated face suddenly became sober. "He was killed on this very mountain. Grandfather never recovered from the shock."

"Oh, I'm so sorry," murmured Penny sympathetically.

"It happened ten years ago while my father was skiing. Ever since then Grandfather has had an almost fanatical hatred of the hotel people. And he is deathly afraid I'll get hurt in some way. He forbids me to ski even on the easy slopes."

"But you do it anyway?"

"Of course. I slip away whenever I can," Sara admitted cheerfully. "Skiing is in my blood. I couldn't give it up."

"And you don't mind deceiving your grandfather?"

"You don't understand. There's no reasoning with him. Each year he gets a little more set in his ways. He knows that I slip away to ski, and that's why he locks me up. Otherwise, Grandfather is a dear. He's taken care of me since my father died."

Sara wriggled into her awkward-fitting coat, wrapped a red scarf about her throat and started for the door.

"Coming, Penny?"

"I haven't promised yet that I will help you get back into your cubby-hole."

"But you will," said Sara confidently.

"I suppose so," sighed Penny. "Nevertheless, I don't particularly like this."

They stepped out of the cabin into the blinding sunlight. The storm had stopped, but the wind blew a gust of snow from the roof into their faces.

"My skis are hidden in the woods," said Sara. "We'll walk along the fence so my footprints won't be so noticeable."

"The place is pretty well marked up now," Penny observed dryly. "Your grandfather would have to be blind not to see them."

"Yes, but they're your tracks, not mine," grinned Sara. "Besides, this strong wind is starting to drift the snow."

They followed the barbed wire fence to the woods. Sara went straight to an old log and from its hollow interior drew out a pair of hickory jumping skis.

"Let's walk up to Mrs. Downey's lodge," she proposed. "Her chute is a dandy, but most of the guests are afraid to use it."

"I haven't tried it myself," admitted Penny. "It looks higher than Pike's Peak."

"Oh, you have plenty of nerve," returned Sara carelessly. "I saw you take Grandfather's barbed wire entanglements."

"That was a matter of necessity."

"Nothing ventured, nothing gained," laughed Sara, linking arms with Penny and pulling her along at a fast pace. "I'll teach you a few tricks."

They climbed the slope steadily until forced to pause for a moment to catch their breath.

"Mrs. Downey isn't using the bob-sled run this year, is she?" Sara inquired curiously.

"I didn't know anything about it."

"She has a fine one on her property, but it's out of sight from the lodge. I guess there haven't been enough guests this season to make it worth while. Too bad. Bob-sled racing is even more fun than skiing."

Coming within view of the Downey lodge, Penny observed that a few of the more hardy guests had taken advantage of the lull in the storm, and were out on the slopes, falling, picking themselves up, falling again.

"I have to run into the house a minute," Penny excused herself. "I'll be right back."

Behind the Green Door

She found Mrs. Downey in the kitchen and reported to her that she had been unable to purchase papers in the village.

"The plane came in, didn't it?"

"Yes, but for some reason the papers weren't put on."

"I wonder if the Fergus hotel managed to get any?"

"I don't see how they could."

"It's happened before," declared Mrs. Downey.

"Time after time we miss our papers, and then I learn later that the Fergus hotel guests had them. I don't understand it, Penny."

"Shall I tell Mr. Glasser?"

"I'll do it," sighed Mrs. Downey. "He's going to be more irritated than ever now."

Penny went outside to find Sara waiting impatiently for her. The girl had strapped on her skis, and was using two sharp-pointed sticks for poles.

"Ready to try the jump, Penny?"

"No, but I'll watch you."

"There's nothing to it, Penny," encouraged Sara as they climbed side by side. "Just keep relaxed and be sure to have your skis pointing upward while you're in the air."

As it became evident that the girls intended to try the chute, a little crowd of spectators gathered on the slope below to watch.

"I'll go first," said Sara, "and after I've landed, you come after me."

"I'll think it over," shivered Penny.

"Don't think too long, or you'll never try it. Just start."

Sara bent to examine her bindings. Then in a graceful crouch she shot down the hill and with a lifting of her arms soared over the take-off. She made a perfectly poised figure in mid-air and an effortless landing on the slope below, finishing off with a christiana turn.

"She's *good!*" thought Penny. "I'll try it, too, even if they carry me off on a stretcher!"

In a wave of enthusiasm she pushed off, keeping her arms behind her. As the edge of the chute loomed up, she swung them forward and sprang into the air. But something went wrong. In an instant she was off balance, her arms swinging wildly in a futile attempt to straighten her body into position.

The gully appeared to be miles below her. Panic surged over Penny and her muscles became rigid. She was going to take a hard fall.

"Relax! Relax!" screamed a shrill voice.

With a supreme effort Penny drew back one ski and bent her knees. She felt a hard jar, and in amazement realized that she had landed on her feet. Her elation was short lived, for the next instant she collapsed and went sliding on down the slope.

Sara ran to help her up.

"Hurt?"

"Not a bit," laughed Penny. "What a spectacle I must have made!"

"Your jump wasn't half bad. Next time you'll do much better."

"I'll never make one as good as yours," Penny said enviously. Seeing Francine standing near, she turned to the reporter and exclaimed: "Did you watch Sara's jump? Wasn't it magnificent?"

"You're both lucky you weren't injured." Francine walked over to the two girls. She stared at Sara's odd looking costume. "You're not a guest here?" she inquired.

"No," answered Sara.

"Nor at the Fergus hotel?"

"I live a ways down the mountain."

Francine regarded her coldly. "You're the Jasko girl, aren't you, whose grandfather will not allow skiers on his property?"

"Yes, but—"

"Since you Jaskos are so sign conscious I should think you might obey them yourself! Take a glance at that one over on the tree. Unless my eyesight is failing it reads: 'Only guests of the hotel may use these slopes.'"

***

CHAPTER 11

A NEWSPAPER MYSTERY

Penny stared at Francine, for a moment not believing that she had meant the remark seriously. As she comprehended that the girl indeed was serious, she exclaimed in quick protest:

"Oh, Francine, what an attitude to take! Sara is my guest. I'm sure Mrs. Downey doesn't mind."

"I'll go," offered Sara in a quiet voice. "I never dreamed I would offend anyone by being here."

"I'm not particularly offended," replied Francine defensively. "It merely seems reasonable to me that if you won't allow others on your property you shouldn't trespass yourself."

"Sara had nothing to do with that sign on her grandfather's land," declared Penny. "Francine, you must have jumped out of the wrong side of the bed this morning."

Sara had turned to walk away. Penny caught her hand, trying to detain her.

"Wait, I'll run into the lodge and ask Mrs. Downey. But I know very well it will be all right for you to stay."

Sara hesitated, and might have consented, save at that instant the three girls heard the faint tinkle of bells. A sled loaded with wood came into view around a curve of the mountain road.

"That's grandfather on his way home!" exclaimed Sara. "I must get back there before he learns I've been away! Hurry, Penny!"

Behind the Green Door

With several quick thrusts of her sticks, she started down the trail which led to the Jasko cabin. Penny followed, but she could not overtake her companion. Sara skied with a reckless skill which defied imitation. While Penny was forced to stem, she took the rough track with no perceptible slackening of speed, and had divested herself of skis by the time her companion reached the woods.

"We'll have to work fast," she warned, hiding the long runners in the hollow log. "I want you to lock me in the cabin and then get away before Grandfather sees you!"

"What about our tracks in the snow?"

"I'll blame them all on you," laughed Sara, "It's beginning to get dark now. And Grandfather is near sighted."

"I don't like this business at all," complained Penny as they kept close to the fence on their way to the cabin. "Why not tell your grandfather—"

"He would rage for days and never let me out again. No, this is the best way. And you'll come back soon, won't you, Penny?"

"I don't like to promise."

"I'll teach you how to jump." Sara offered attractive bait.

"We'll see. I'll think it over."

"No, promise!" persisted Sara. "Say you'll come back and at least talk to me through the window. You have no idea how lonesome I get."

"All right," Penny suddenly gave in. "I'll do that much."

Reaching the cabin, Sara had Penny tramp about in the snow with her skis so as to give the impression that a visitor had walked several times around the building but had not entered.

"You'll have to lock me in the loft," she instructed. "Then take the key back to the woodshed and get away as quickly as you can."

Sara pulled off her garments and hung them in the closet. With a mop she wiped up tracks which had been made on the bare floor. Then she climbed up the ladder to her room.

Penny turned the wooden peg, and retreating from the cabin, locked the door.

"Don't forget!" Sara called to her from the window. "Come again soon—tomorrow if you can."

Hiding the key in the woodshed, Penny tramped about the outside of the building several times before gliding off toward the boundary fence. As she began a tedious climb up the trail toward the Downey lodge, she saw the sled appear around a bend of the road.

Penny did not visit the Jasko cabin the following day nor the next. Along with other guests she was kept indoors by a raging snow and sleet storm which blocked the road and disrupted telephone service to the village.

Everyone at the Downey lodge suffered from the confinement, but some accepted the situation more philosophically than others. As usual Mr. Glasser complained because there were no daily papers. Penny overheard him telling another guest he was thinking very seriously of moving to the Fergus hotel where at least a certain amount of entertainment was provided.

"He'll leave," Mrs. Downey observed resignedly when the conversation was repeated to her. "I've seen it coming for days. Mr. Glasser has been talking with one of the runners for the Fergus hotel."

"It's unfair of them to try to take your guests away."

"Oh, they're determined to put me out of business at any cost. Miss Sellberg is leaving, too. She served notice this morning."

Penny glanced up with quick interest. "Francine? Is she leaving Pine Top?"

"No, she told me she had decided to move to the Fergus hotel because of its better location."

Penny nodded thoughtfully. She could understand that if Francine were trying to gain special information about either Ralph Fergus or Harvey Maxwell, it would be to her advantage to have a room at the other hotel. Had it not been for her loyalty to Mrs. Downey, she, too, would have been tempted to take up headquarters there.

                                    Behind the Green Door

"I can't really blame folks for leaving," Mrs. Downey continued after a moment. "I've not offered very much entertainment this year. Last season in addition to skiing we had the bob-sled run."

"I met Sara Jasko and she was telling me about it," replied Penny. "Can't you use the run again this year?"

"We could, but it scarcely seems worth the trouble and expense. Also, it takes experienced drivers to steer the sleds. The young man I had working for me last winter isn't available at present."

"Is there no other person at Pine Top who could do it?"

"Sara Jasko," responded Mrs. Downey, smiling. "However, it's not likely her grandfather would give his consent."

The following day dawned bright and clear and brought a revival of spirit at the Downey lodge. Nevertheless, with the roads open once more, both Francine and Mr. Glasser moved their belongings down to the Fergus hotel. As was to be expected, their departure caused a certain amount of comment by the other guests.

Late in the afternoon Penny offered to ski down to Pine Top for the newspapers. She planned to stop at the Fergus hotel upon her return, hoping to learn a little more about the mysterious Green Room which had intrigued her interest.

Reaching the village, Penny located Benny Smith, but the lad shook his head when she inquired for the daily papers.

"I don't have any today."

"But the plane came through! I saw it myself about an hour ago. This makes four days since we've had a newspaper at the lodge. What happened?"

The boy glared at Penny almost defiantly. "You can't blame me. It's not my fault if they're not put on the plane."

"No, of course not. I didn't mean to suggest that you were at fault. It's just queer that we miss our papers so often. And we never seem to get the back editions either."

"Well, I don't know anything about it," the boy muttered.

Penny stood watching him slouch off down the street. Something about the lad's manner made her wonder if he had not lied. She suddenly was convinced that Benny knew more about the missing newspapers than he cared to tell.

"But how would he profit by not receiving them?" she mused. "He would lose sales. It simply doesn't make sense."

As she trudged on down the street Penny turned the problem over in her mind. She walked with head bent low and did not notice an approaching pedestrian until she had bumped into him.

"Sorry," apologized the man politely.

"It was my fault," replied Penny. She glanced up to see that the stranger was no stranger at all, but the airplane pilot who had brought her to Pine Top several days before.

He would have passed on had she not halted him with a question.

"I wonder if you could tell me what seems to be the trouble with the newspaper delivery service here at Pine Top?"

"We couldn't get through yesterday on account of the weather," he returned.

"But what happened to the papers today?"

"Nothing."

"You mean they came through?" Penny asked in surprise.

"That's right. You can get them from Benny Smith."

"From Benny? But he said—"

Penny started to reveal that the boy had blamed the failure of service upon the pilot, and then changed her mind.

"Thank you," she returned, "I'll talk with him."

Penny was more puzzled than ever, but she had no reason to doubt the pilot's word. Obviously, the newspapers had arrived at Pine Top, and Benny Smith knew what had become of them.

"I'll just investigate this matter a little further," Penny decided as she left the village.

Approaching the Fergus hotel a few minutes later, she paused to catch her breath before going inside. In the gathering twilight the building looked more than ever like a great Swiss chalet. The pitched roof was burdened with a thick layer of white snow, and long icicles hung from the window ledges.

Inside the crowded, smoke-filled lobby there was an air of gaiety. A few lights had been turned on, and the orchestra could be heard tuning up in the dining room.

Penny saw no one that she knew. Crossing quickly to a counter at the far side of the lobby, she spoke to a girl who was in charge.

"Can I buy a newspaper here?"

"Yes, we have them." The girl reached around a corner of the counter, indicating a stack of papers which Penny had not seen. "New York Times?"

"That will do very nicely."

Penny paid for the paper and carrying it over to a chair, quickly looked at the dateline.

"It's today's issue, all right," she told herself grimly. "This proves what I suspected. Ralph Fergus has been buying up all the papers—a little trick to annoy Mrs. Downey and get her in bad with her guests!"

***

CHAPTER 12

THE GREEN CARD

"Do you always talk to yourself?" inquired an amused voice from behind Penny.

Glancing up from the newspaper, the girl saw Maxine Miller standing beside her chair. For an instant she failed to recognize the actress, so elegant did the woman appear in a sealskin coat and matching hat. The outfit was so new that the fur had lost none of its glaze, an observation which caused Penny to wonder if Miss Miller had misled her regarding the state of her finances.

"Good evening, Miss Miller," she smiled. "I didn't know you for a moment."

"How do you like it?" inquired the actress, turning slowly about.

"Your new fur coat? It's very beautiful. And you're looking well, too. You didn't by chance get that role from David Balantine?"

Miss Miller's painted lips drew into a pout. "No, he left the hotel this morning."

"Oh, that's too bad. I suppose you'll be going soon, then?"

The actress shook her head, and laughed in a mysterious way.

"No, I've decided to stay here for awhile. I like Pine Top."

Penny was puzzled by Miss Miller's sudden change in manner and appearance. The woman acted as if she were the possessor of an important secret which she longed to reveal.

"You must have fallen heiress to a vast fortune," Penny ventured lightly.

"Better than that," beamed Miss Miller. "I've acquired a new job. Take dinner with me and I'll tell you all about it."

"Well—" Penny deliberated and said honestly, "I didn't bring very much money with me, and I'm not dressed up."

Miss Miller brushed aside both objections as if they were of no consequence.

"You'll be my guest, dearie. And your clothes don't matter."

She caught Penny's hand and pulled her to her feet. Her curiosity aroused, the girl allowed herself to be escorted to the dining room.

Miss Miller walked ahead, strutting a bit as she brushed past the crowded tables. Heads lifted and envious feminine eyes focused upon the actress' stunning fur coat. Penny felt awkward and embarrassed, clomping along behind in her big heavy ski boots.

The head waiter gave them a choice table near the orchestra. Miss Miller threw back her coat, exposing a form-fitting black satin gown with a brilliant blue stone pin at the neck line. She knew that she was creating an impression and thoroughly enjoyed herself.

A waiter brought menu cards. The actress proceeded to order for both herself and Penny. She selected the most expensive dishes offered, stumbling over their long French names.

"How nice it is to have money again," she remarked languidly when the waiter had gone. "Do you really like my new wardrobe, dearie?"

"Indeed, I do, Miss Miller. Your dress is very becoming, and the fur coat is stunning. Isn't it new?"

"Exactly two days old."

"Then you must have acquired it since coming to Pine Top. I had no idea such lovely skins could be bought anywhere near here."

"We're very close to the Canadian border, you know." Again the actress flashed her mysterious smile. "But the duty is frightful unless one is able to avoid it."

Penny gazed thoughtfully across the table at her companion.

"And do you know how to avoid it?" she asked as casually as she could manage.

Miss Miller steered skilfully away from the subject.

"Oh, this coat was given to me. It didn't cost me a cent."

"And how does one go about acquiring a free coat? You've not become a professional model?"

"No," the actress denied, "but your guess is fairly warm. I do have a nice figure for displaying clothes. No doubt that was why I was given the job."

"Who is your employer, Miss Miller? Someone connected with the hotel?"

The waiter had brought a loaded tray to the table, and the actress used his arrival as a pretext for not answering Penny's question. After the man went away she began to chat glibly about other subjects. However, with the serving of dessert, she once more switched to the topic of her wardrobe.

"You were asking me about my fur coat, dearie," she said. "Would you like to have one like it?"

"Who wouldn't? What must I do to acquire one—rob a bank?"

Miss Miller laughed in a forced way. "You will have your little joke. From what you've told me, I imagine your father has plenty of money."

"I don't remember saying anything about it," responded Penny dryly. "As a matter of fact, my father isn't wealthy."

"At least your family is comfortably fixed or you wouldn't be at this expensive winter resort," Miss Miller went on, undisturbed. "Now would you be able to pay as much as a hundred dollars for a coat?"

"I hadn't even thought of buying one," replied Penny, trying not to disclose her astonishment. "Can you really get a good fur coat for as little as a hundred dollars?"

"You could through my friend."

"Your friend?" asked Penny bluntly. "Do you mean your new employer?"

"Well, yes," the actress admitted with a self-conscious laugh. "He is a fur salesman. You've been very nice to me and I might be able to get a coat for you at cost."

"That's most kind," remarked Penny dryly. "Where could I see these coats?"

"My employer has a salesroom here at the hotel," Miss Miller declared. "I can arrange an appointment for you. Say tomorrow at two?"

"I haven't enough money with me to buy a coat even if I wanted one."

"But if you liked the furs you could wire your parents for more," the actress wheedled. "It is a wonderful opportunity. You'll never have another chance to buy a beautiful coat at cost."

"I'll have to think it over," Penny returned. "I suppose you get a commission on every garment sold?"

"A small one. In your case, I'll not take it. I truly am interested in seeing you get your coat, dearie. You have just the figure for it, you're so slim and svelte."

Penny was not deceived by the flattery. She knew very well that the actress had treated her to dinner for the purpose of making her feel under obligation and as a build-up to the suggestion that she purchase a fur coat.

Glancing at the bill she was relieved to see that she had enough money to pay for her share of the meal.

"No, no, I won't hear of it," Miss Miller protested grandly.

Summoning the waiter, she gave him a twenty dollar bill.

"Let me know if you decide you would like to see the coats," she said to Penny as they left the dining room together. "It won't cost you anything to look, you know."

"I'll think it over. Thanks for the dinner."

Penny looked about the crowded lobby for Ralph Fergus or Harvey Maxwell, but neither man was to be seen. While at the hotel she would have liked to acquire a little more information about the Green Room. With the actress hovering at her elbow it was out of the question.

She considered speaking of the matter to Miss Miller, and then abandoned the idea. However, it had occurred to her that the mysterious room of the hotel might have some connection with the actress' present employment, and so she ventured one rather direct question.

"Miss Miller, you're not by chance working for Ralph Fergus or the hotel?"

"Dear me, no!" the actress denied. "Whatever put such an idea in your head?"

"It just occurred to me. Well, good-bye."

Penny left the hotel and ventured out into the cold. After so much cigarette smoke, the pure air was a pleasant relief. She broke off a long icicle from the doorway, and stood thoughtfully chewing at it.

"Miss Miller must be working for some dishonest outfit," she mused. "Her talk about getting a fur coat at cost doesn't fool me one bit. If I were in her shoes I'd be more than a little worried lest I tangled with the law."

A remark by the actress to the effect that the Canadian border was close by had set Penny's active mind to working. It was not too fantastic to believe that Miss Miller might be employed by an unscrupulous man whose business concerned the sale of furs obtained duty free. She had even dared hope that Ralph Fergus or Harvey Maxwell might be implicated in the dishonest affair. What a break that would be for her father if only she could prove such a connection! But the actress' outright denial that either man was her employer had put an end to such pleasant speculation.

Penny bent down to pick up her skis which had been left at the side of the hotel building. As she leaned over, she noticed a small object lying on top of the snow in the square of light made from one of the windows. It appeared to be a small piece of colored cardboard.

Curiously, Penny picked it up and carried it closer to the window. The card was green. Her pulse quickened as she turned it over. On its face were six engraved words:

"Admit Bearer Through The Green Door."

***

CHAPTER 13

AN UNKIND TRICK

Penny all but executed a clog dance in the snow. She knew that she had picked up an admittance ticket to the Green Room of the Fergus hotel which some person had lost. With no effort upon her part she would be able to learn the answer to many of the questions which had plagued her.

"At last I'll find out what lies behind that Green Door," she thought in high elation. "If this isn't the most wonderful piece of luck!"

Debating a moment, Penny decided that it probably was too late to gain admittance that evening. Mrs. Downey no doubt was worried over her long absence from the lodge. She would return there, and then revisit the hotel early the next day.

Pocketing the precious ticket, Penny set off up the mountain. It was dark before she had covered half the distance, but there were stars and a half moon to guide her.

Mrs. Downey showed her relief as the girl stomped into the kitchen.

"I was beginning to worry, Penny," she declared. "Whatever made it take you so long?"

"I stopped at the Fergus hotel and had dinner with Miss Miller."

"Were you able to get the newspapers?"

"Only one which I had to buy at the Fergus hotel. Mrs. Downey, it's queer about those papers. Benny Smith told me there weren't any to be had, and then a few minutes later I met the airplane pilot who told me he had brought them in the same as usual. Also, the Fergus hotel received its usual quota."

"Well, that's odd."

"It looks to me as if the Fergus outfit has made some arrangement with the paper boy. They may be buying up all the papers."

"As a means of annoying me," nodded Mrs. Downey grimly. "It would be in line with their tactics. But what can I do?"

"I don't know," admitted Penny. She pulled off her heavy boots and set them where they would dry. "We haven't any proof they're doing anything like that. It's only my idea."

The door opened and Jake came into the kitchen. He dropped an armload of wood behind the range.

"I started work on the bob-sled run this afternoon," he remarked to Mrs. Downey. "Got a crew of boys coming first thing tomorrow. We ought to have her fixed up by noon."

"And the sleds?"

"They seem to be in good condition, but I'll check everything."

After the workman had gone, Penny glanced questioningly at Mrs. Downey.

"Have you decided to use the run after all?"

"Yes, I started thinking about it after we talked together. We do need more entertainment here at the lodge. After you left I ordered Jake to start work on the track. But I still am in need of experienced drivers for the sled."

"You spoke of Sara."

"I thought I would ask her, but I doubt if her Grandfather will give his consent."

"I'll ski down there tomorrow and talk with her if you would like me to," offered Penny.

"I would appreciate it," said Mrs. Downey gratefully. "I hate to spare the time myself."

Early the next morning Penny paid a visit to the bob-sled run where a crew headed by Jake was hard at work. There was a stretch of straightaway and a series of curves which snaked down the valley between the pines. At the point of the steepest curve, the outer snow walls rose to a height of eighteen feet.

"A sled could really travel on that track," observed Penny. "Does it hurt to upset?"

"It might," grinned Jake. "We've never had an upset on Horseshoe Curve. If a sled went over there, you might wake up in the hospital."

Penny watched the men packing snow for awhile. Then buckling on her skis, she made a fast trip down the mountain to the Jasko cabin. This time, having a definite mission, she went boldly to the door and rapped.

There was no response until the window of the loft shot up.

"Hello, Penny," called down Sara. "I thought you had forgotten your promise. The key's in the same place."

"Isn't your grandfather here?"

"No, he went down to Pine Top. Isn't it glorious skiing weather? Hurry and get the key. I've been cooped up here half an hour already."

Penny went reluctantly to the woodshed and returned with the key. She unfastened the trapdoor which gave entrance to the loft and Sara quickly descended.

"Didn't your grandfather say anything about last time?" Penny inquired anxiously.

"Oh, he raved because someone had trespassed. But it never occurred to him I had gone away. Where shall we ski today?"

"I only stopped to deliver a message, Sara. I am on my way down to the Fergus hotel."

"Oh," said the girl in disappointment. "A message from whom?"

"Mrs. Downey. She is starting up her bob-sled run again and she wants you to help out."

Sara's eyes began to sparkle.

"I wish I could! If only Grandfather weren't so strict."

"Is there a chance he'll give his consent?"

"Oh, dear, no. But I might be able to slip away. Grandfather plans to chop wood every day this week."

"I doubt if Mrs. Downey would want you to do that."

"Need you tell her?" queried Sara coolly. "I'll fix myself a rope ladder and get out the window. That will save you the trouble of coming here to let me in and out."

"And what will your grandfather say if he learns about it?"

"Plenty! But anything is better than being shut up like a prisoner. You tell Mrs. Downey I'll try to get up to the lodge tomorrow morning, and we'll try out the track together, eh Penny?"

"I don't know anything about bob-sledding."

"I'll teach you to be my brake boy," Sara laughed. "How long will you stay at the Fergus hotel?"

"I haven't any idea."

"Then I suppose I'll have to crawl back into my cave," Sara sighed dismally. "Can't you even ski with me for half an hour?"

"Not this morning," Penny said firmly. "I have important work ahead."

She shooed Sara back into the loft and returned the key to the woodshed. The Jasko girl watched from the window, playfully shaking her fist as her friend skied away.

"Sara is as stimulating as a mountain avalanche," chuckled Penny, "but she's almost too headstrong. Sooner or later her stunts will involve me in trouble with Peter Jasko."

In the valley below, smoke curled lazily from the chimneys of the Fergus hotel. Making directly for it, Penny felt in her pocket to be certain she had not lost the green ticket which she had found the previous evening.

"This is going to be my lucky day," she told herself cheerfully. "I feel it in my bones."

                                    Behind the Green Door

Reaching the hotel, Penny stripped off her skis and entered the hotel lobby. Maxine Miller was not in evidence nor did she see any other person who likely would question her presence there. She did notice Harvey Maxwell sitting in the private office. His eyes were upon her as she crossed the room. However, Penny felt no uneasiness, realizing that if he noticed her at all he recognized her only as a guest at the Downey lodge.

"Second floor," she said quietly to the elevator boy.

Penny was the sole passenger, but as she stepped from the cage, she was dismayed to run directly into Francine Sellberg.

The reporter greeted her with a suspicious stare.

"Why, hello, Penny Parker. What are you doing here?"

"Oh, just moseying around."

"I can see you are!"

"Your room isn't on this floor, is it?" Penny inquired.

"No, on the fourth," Francine answered before she considered her words.

"Looking for someone?" remarked Penny with a grin. "Or should I say *something*?"

An elevator stopped at the landing. "Going down," the attendant called, opening the door. He gazed questioningly at the two girls.

Francine shook her head, although she had been waiting for an elevator. Turning again to Penny she said with a hard smile: "I've not only been looking for something, I've found it!"

"Still, I don't see you rushing to reach a telephone, Francine. Your discovery can't have such tremendous news value."

"It may have before long," hinted Francine. "I don't mind telling you I am on the trail of a really big story. And I am making steady progress in assembling my facts."

Penny regarded the girl reporter speculatively. Her presence on the second floor rather suggested that she, too, had been trying to investigate the Green Room, and more than likely had learned its location. But she was reasonably certain Francine had gathered no information of great value.

"Glad to hear you're doing so well," she remarked and started on down the hall.

Francine fell into step with her. "If you're looking for a particular room, Penny, maybe I can help you."

Penny knew that the reporter meant to stay with her so that she could do no investigation work of her own.

"The room I am searching for has a green door," she replied.

Francine laughed. "I'm glad you're so honest, Penny. I guessed why you were on this floor all the time. However, I greatly fear you're in the wrong part of the hotel."

Penny paused and turned to face her companion squarely. "Why not put an end to all this nonsense, Francine? We watch each other and get nowhere. Let's put our cards on the table."

"Yours might be a joker!"

"We're both interested in getting a story which will discredit Harvey Maxwell," Penny went on, ignoring the jibe. "You've had a tip as to what may be going on here, while I'm working in the dark. On the other hand, I've acquired something which should interest you. Why don't we pool our interests and work together?"

"That would be very nice—for you."

"I think I might contribute something to the case."

"I doubt it," replied Francine loftily. "You don't even know the location of the Green Room."

"You're wrong about that. It took no great detective power to learn it's on this floor. To get inside may be a different matter."

"You're quite right there," said Francine with emphasis.

"What do you say? Shall we work together and let bygones be bygones?"

"Thank you, Penny, I prefer to work alone."

"Suit yourself, Francine. I was only trying to be generous. You see, I have an admittance card to the Green Room."

"I don't believe it!"

Flashing a gay smile, Penny held up the ticket for Francine to see.

"How did you get it?" the reporter gasped. "I've tried—"

"A little bird dropped it on my window sill. Too bad you didn't decide to work with me."

Penny walked on down the corridor, and Francine made no attempt to follow. When she glanced back over her shoulder the reporter had descended the stairway to the lobby.

"It was boastful of me to show her my ticket," she thought. "But I couldn't resist doing it. Francine is so conceited."

Making her way to the unmarked door of the wing, Penny paused there a moment, listening. Hearing no sound she pushed open the door and went down the narrow hall. The guard sat at his usual post before the Green Door.

"Good morning," said Penny pleasantly. "I have my card now."

The man examined it and handed it back. "Go right in," he told her.

Before Penny could obey, the door at the end of the corridor swung open. Harvey Maxwell, his face convulsed with rage, came hurrying toward the startled girl.

"I've just learned who you are," he said angrily. "Kindly leave this hotel at once, and don't come back!"

***

CHAPTER 14

A BROKEN ROD

"You must have mistaken me for some other person," Penny stammered, backing a step away from the hotel man. "Who do you think I am?"

The question was a mistake, for it only served to intensify Harvey Maxwell's anger.

"You're the daughter of Anthony Parker who runs the yellowest paper in Riverview! I know why he sent you here. Now get out and don't let me catch you in the hotel ever again."

Observing the green card in Penny's hand he reached out and jerked it from her.

"I wasn't doing any harm," she said, trying to act injured. "My father didn't send me to Pine Top. I came for the skiing."

Secretly, Penny was angry at Maxwell's reference to the *Riverview Star* as being a "yellow" sheet, which in newspaper jargon meant that it was a sensation-seeking newspaper.

"And what are you doing in this part of the hotel?"

"I only wanted to see the Green Room," Penny replied. "I thought I would have my breakfast here."

Harvey Maxwell and the doorman exchanged a quick glance which was not lost upon the girl.

"Where did you get your ticket?" the hotel man demanded but in a less harsh voice.

"I picked it up outside the hotel."

Penny spoke truthfully and her words carried conviction. Harvey Maxwell seemed satisfied that she had not been investigating the wing for any special purpose. However, he took her by an elbow and steered her down the corridor to the elevator.

"If you're the smart little girl I think you are, a hint will be sufficient," he said. "I don't want any member of the Parker family on my premises. So stay away. Get me?"

"Yes, sir," responded Penny meekly.

Inwardly, she was raging. Someone deliberately had betrayed her to Harvey Maxwell and she had a very good idea who that person might be. From now on employes of the hotel would be told to keep watch for her. Never again would she be allowed in the lobby, much less in the vicinity of the Green Room.

Harvey Maxwell walked with Penny to the front door of the hotel and closed it behind her.

"Remember," he warned, "stay away."

As Penny started down the walk she heard a silvery laugh, and glancing sideways, saw Francine leaning against the building.

"You didn't spend much time in the Green Room, did you?" she inquired.

"That was a dirty trick to play!" retorted Penny. "I wouldn't have done it to you."

"You couldn't have thought that fast, my dear Penny."

"I might tell Mr. Maxwell you're a reporter for the *Riverview Record*. How would you like that?"

Francine shrugged. "In that case we both lose the story. All I want is an exclusive. After the yarn breaks in the *Record*, your father will be welcome to make use of any information published. So if you really want him to win his libel suit, you'll gain by not interfering with me."

"You reason in a very strange way," replied Penny coldly.

Picking up her skis she shouldered them and marched stiffly away. She was angry at Francine and angry at herself for having given the rival reporter an opportunity to score against her. Probably she would never tell Harvey Maxwell or Ralph Fergus who the girl actually was, sorely as she might be tempted. As Francine had pointed out, her own chance of gleaning any worth while information had been lost.

"It's a bitter pill to choke down," thought Penny, "but I would rather have the *Record* get the story than to lose it altogether."

Sunk deep in depression, she tramped back to the Downey lodge. The mail had arrived during her absence but there was no letter from home.

"Dad might at least send me a postcard," she grumbled. "For two cents I would take the next plane back to Riverview."

However, Penny could not remain downhearted for any great length of time. Why worry about Francine and the silly old Green Room? She would forget all about it and try to have fun for a change.

It was not difficult to dismiss the matter from her mind, for the following morning Sara Jasko came to give her a lesson in bob-sled driving. With a crowd of interested guests watching from the sidelines, they made their first exciting ride over the track. Sara steered, Jake operated the brake, and Penny rode as sole passenger.

Horseshoe Curve was the most thrilling point on the course. As the sled tore around it at a tremendous rate of speed, Jake dug in the iron claw of the brake, sending up a plume of snow. They slackened speed perceptibly, but even so the sled climbed high on the sloping wall, and Penny thought for an anxious moment that they were going over the top. The remainder of the run was mild by comparison.

Upon later trips Penny was allowed to manage the brake, and soon became dexterous in applying it as Sara shouted the command.

Skiers abandoned the slopes to watch the new sport. Two at a time, Penny and Sara gave them rides and all of their passengers were enthusiastic.

By the following day the word had spread down the mountain that Mrs. Downey's bob-sled run was operating. Guests from the Fergus hotel joined the throng but they were given rides only when there were no passengers waiting.

"It's going over like a house afire!" Penny declared gaily to Mrs. Downey. "I shouldn't be surprised if you take some of the Fergus hotel's customers away from them if this enthusiasm lasts."

"You and Sara are showing folks a wonderful time."

"And we're having one ourselves. It's even more fun than skiing."

"But more dangerous," declared Mrs. Downey. "I hope we have no accidents."

"Sara is a skillful driver."

"Yes, she is," agreed Mrs. Downey. "There's no cause for worry so long as the track isn't icy."

Two days passed during which Penny did not even go near the Fergus hotel or to the village. As she remarked to Mrs. Downey, all of Pine Top came to the lodge. During the morning hours when the bob-sled run was in operation, a long line of passengers stood waiting. Guests from the Fergus hotel had few chances for rides. Several of them, wishing to be on the favored list, checked out and came to take lodging at Mrs. Downey's place.

"I can't understand it," the woman declared to Penny. "Last year the run wasn't very popular. I think it may have been because we had a little accident at the beginning of the season. Nothing serious but it served to frighten folks."

"I wonder how the Fergus-Maxwell interests are enjoying it?" chuckled Penny.

"Not very well, you may be sure. This flurry in our business will rather worry them. They may not put me out of business as quickly as they expected."

"At least you'll end your season in a blaze of glory," laughed Penny.

The weather had turned warmer. Late Thursday afternoon the snow melted a bit and the lowering night temperatures caused a film of ice to form over the entire length of the bob-sled run. Jake shook his head as he talked over the situation with Penny the next morning.

"The track will be fast and slippery this morning."

"A lot of folks will be disappointed if we don't make any trips," declared Penny. "Here comes Sara. Let's see what she has to say."

Sara studied the run, and walked down as far as Horseshoe Curve.

"It's fast all right," she conceded. "But that will only make it the more exciting. Brakes in good order, Jake?"

"I tested every sled last night after they were brought to the shop."

"Then we'll have no trouble," said Sara confidently. "Round up the passengers, Jake, and we'll start at once."

The sled was hauled to the starting line. Sara took her place behind the wheel, with Penny riding the end position to handle the brake. Their first passengers were to be a middle aged married couple. Sara gave them padded helmets to wear.

"What are these for?" the woman asked nervously. "The toboggan slide isn't dangerous, is it?"

"No, certainly not," answered Sara. "We haven't had a spill this year. Hang tight on the curves. Give me plenty of brake when I call for it, Penny."

She signaled for the push off. They started fast and gathered speed on the straightaway. Penny wondered how Sara could steer for her own eyes blurred as they shot down the icy trough. They never had traveled at such high speed before.

"Brakes!" shouted Sara.

Penny obeyed the order, and felt the sled slow down as the brake claw dug into the snow and ice. They raced on toward the first wide curve, and swung around it, high on the banked wall, too close to the outside edge for comfort.

"Brakes!" called Sara again.

Once more the iron claw dug in, sending up a spray of snow behind the racing sled. And then there came a strange, pinging sound.

For the briefest instant Penny did not comprehend its significance. Then, as the sled leaped ahead faster than ever and the geyser of snow vanished, she realized what had happened. The brakes were useless! A rod had snapped! They were roaring down the track with undiminished speed, and Horseshoe Curve, the most dangerous point on the run, lay directly ahead.

***

CHAPTER 15

IN THE TOOL HOUSE

Sara, her face white and tense, turned her head for a fraction of a second and then, crouching lower, kept her eyes glued on the track. She knew what had happened, and she knew, too, that they never could hope to make the Horseshoe Curve. Even a miracle of steering would not save them from going over the wall of ice at terrific speed.

The two passengers, frozen with fright, gripped the side ropes, and kept their heads down. It did not even occur to them that they could save themselves by rolling off. For that matter, they did not realize that the brake had broken.

Penny, in end position, could have jumped easily, A fall into the soft snow beside the track would be far less apt to cause serious injury than an upset from the high wall of the curve. But it never occurred to her to try to save herself.

There was only one slim chance of preventing a bad accident, a costly one for herself, and Penny took it. As the perpendicular wall of Horseshoe Curve loomed up ahead, she wrapped her arm about the side rope of the sled and hurled herself off. Her entire body was given a violent jerk. A sharp pain shot through her right arm, but she gritted her teeth and held on.

Penny's trailing body, acting as a brake, slowed down the sled and kept it from upsetting as it swept into the curve. Sideways it climbed the wall of snow. It crept to the very edge, hovered there a breathless moment, then fell back to overturn at the flat side of the curve.

Untangling herself from a pile of arms and legs, Sara began to help her passengers to their feet.

"Penny, are you hurt?" she asked anxiously. "That was a courageous thing to do! You saved us from a bad accident."

Spectators, thrilled by the display of heroism, came running to the scene. Penny, every muscle screaming with pain, rolled over in the snow. Gripping her wrenched arm, she tried to get to her feet and could not.

"Penny, you *are* hurt!" cried Sara.

"It's my arm, more than anything else," Penny said, trying to keep her face from twisting. "I—I hope it's not broken."

Willing hands raised her to her feet and supported her. Penny was relieved to discover that she could lift her injured arm.

"It's only wrenched," she murmured. "Anyone else hurt, Sara?"

"You're the only casualty," Sara replied warmly. "But if you hadn't used yourself as a brake we might all have been badly injured. You ought to get a hot bath as quickly as you can before your muscles begin to stiffen."

"They've begun already," replied Penny ruefully.

She took a step as if to start for the lodge, only to hesitate.

"I wonder what happened to the brake? I heard something give way."

Sara overturned the sled and took one glance. "A broken rod."

"I thought Jake checked over everything last night."

"That's what he *said*," returned Sara. "We'll ask him about it."

The workman, white-faced and frightened, came running down the hill.

"What happened?" he demanded. "Couldn't you slow down or was it too icy?"

"No brakes," Sara answered laconically. "I thought you tested them."

"I did. They were in good order last night."

"Take a look at this." Sara pointed to the broken rod.

Jake bent down to examine it. When he straightened he spoke no word, but the expression of his face told the two girls that he did not hold himself responsible for the mishap.

"There's something funny about this," he muttered. "I'll take the sled to the shop and have a look at it."

"I'll go along with you," declared Sara.

"And so will I," added Penny quickly.

"You really should get a hot bath and go to bed," advised Sara. "If you don't you may not be able to walk tomorrow."

"I'll go to bed in a little while," Penny answered significantly.

Followed by the two girls, Jake pulled the sled to the tool house behind the lodge. Sara immediately closed and bolted the door from the inside so that curious persons would not enter.

"Now let's really have a look at that brake rod," she said. "Notice anything queer about it, Penny?"

"I did, and I'm thinking the same thing you are."

"See these shiny marks on the steel," Jake pointed out excitedly. "The rod had been sawed almost in two. Even a little strain on it would make it break."

"You're certain it was in good condition last night?" Sara questioned.

"Positive," Jake responded grimly. "I checked over both sleds just before supper last night."

"Let's have a look at the other sled," proposed Penny.

An inspection of the brake equipment revealed nothing out of order.

"Whoever did the trick may have been afraid to damage both sleds for fear of drawing attention to his criminal work," declared Penny. "But it's perfectly evident someone wanted us to take a bad spill."

"I can't guess who would try such a trick," said Sara in perplexity. "Did you lock the tool house last night, Jake?"

"I always do."

"How about the windows?" inquired Penny.

"I don't rightly remember," Jake confessed. "I reckon they're stuck fast."

Penny went over and tested one of the windows. While it was not locked, she could not raise it with her injured arm. Sara tried without any better luck.

However, as the girls examined the one on the opposite side of the tool house, they discovered that it raised and lowered readily. Tiny pieces of wood were chipped from the outside sill, showing where a blunt instrument had been inserted beneath the sash.

"This is where the person entered, all right," declared Penny.

"I can't understand who would wish to injure us," said Sara in a baffled voice. "You're not known here at Pine Top, and I have no enemies to my knowledge."

"Mrs. Downey has them. There are persons who would like to see her out of business. And our bob-sledding parties were growing popular."

"They were taking a few guests away from the big hotel," Sara admitted slowly. "Still, it doesn't seem possible—"

She broke off as Penny reached down to pick up a small object which lay on the floor beneath the window.

"What have you found?" she finished quickly.

Penny held out a large black button for her to see. A few strands of coarse dark thread still clung to the eyelets.

"It looks like a button from a man's overcoat!" exclaimed Sara. "Jake, does this belong to you?"

The workman glanced at it and shook his head.

"Not mine."

"It probably fell from the coat of the person who damaged our sled," Penny declared thoughtfully. "Not much of a clue, perhaps, but at least it's something to go on!"

***

CHAPTER 16

A PUZZLING SOLUTION

Penny pocketed the button and then with Sara went outside the building to look for additional clues. The girls found only a multitude of footprints in the snow beneath the two windows, for the tool house stood beside a direct path to the nursery slopes.

"We've learned everything we're going to," declared Sara. "Penny, I do wish you would get into the house and take your bath. You're limping worse every minute."

"All right, I'll go. I do feel miserable."

"Perhaps you ought to have a doctor."

Penny laughed in amusement. "I'll be brake man on the bob-sled tomorrow as usual."

"You'll be lucky if you're able to crawl out of bed. Anyway, I doubt if I'll be able to come myself."

"Your grandfather?" asked Penny quickly.

"Yes, he's getting suspicious. I'll have to be more careful."

"Why don't you tell him the truth? It's really not fair to deceive him. He's bound to learn the truth sooner or later."

"I'm afraid to tell him," Sara said with a little shiver. "When grandfather is angry you can't reason with him. I'll have to run now. I'm later than usual."

Penny watched her friend go and then hobbled into the lodge. News of the accident had preceded her, and Mrs. Downey met her at the door. She was deeply troubled until she ascertained for herself that the girl had not been seriously injured.

"I was afraid something like this would happen," Mrs. Downey murmured self accusingly. "You know now why I wasn't very enthusiastic about using the bob-sled run."

Penny decided not to tell Mrs. Downey until later how the mishap had occurred. She was feeling too miserable to do much talking, and she knew the truth would only add to the woman's worries.

"I can't say I'm so thrilled about it myself at the moment," she declared with a grimace. "I feel as stiff as if I were mounted on a mummy board!"

Mrs. Downey drew a tub of hot water, but it required all of Penny's athletic prowess to get herself in and out of it. Her right arm was swollen and painful to lift. The skin on one side of her body from hip to ankle had been severely scraped and bruised. She could turn her neck only with difficulty.

"I do think I should call a doctor from the village," Mrs. Downey declared as she aided the girl into bed.

"Please, don't," pleaded Penny. "I'll be as frisky as ever by tomorrow."

Mrs. Downey lowered the shades and went away. Left alone, Penny tried to go to sleep, but she was too uncomfortable. Every time she shifted to a new position wracking pains shot through her body.

"If this isn't the worst break," she thought, sinking deep into gloom. "I'll be crippled for several days at least. No skiing, no bob-sledding. And while I'm lying here on my bed of pain, Francine will learn all about the Green Room."

After awhile the warmth of the bed overcame Penny and she slept. She awakened to find Mrs. Downey standing beside her, a tray in her hand.

"I shouldn't have disturbed you," the woman apologized, "but you've been sleeping so long. And you've had nothing to eat."

"I could do with a little luncheon," mumbled Penny drowsily. "You didn't need to bother bringing it upstairs."

"This is dinner, not luncheon," corrected Mrs. Downey.

Penny rolled over and painfully pulled herself to a sitting posture.

"Then I must have slept hours! What time is it?"

"Five-thirty. Do you feel better, Penny?"

"I think I do. From my eyebrows up anyway."

While Penny ate her dinner, Mrs. Downey sat beside her and chatted.

"At least there's nothing wrong with my appetite," the girl laughed, rapidly emptying the dishes. "At home Mrs. Weems says I eat like a wolf. Oh, by the way, any mail?"

"None for you."

Penny's face clouded. "It's funny no one writes me. Don't you think I might at least get an advertising circular?"

"Well, Christmas is coming," Mrs. Downey said reasonably. "The holiday season always is such a busy time. Folks have their shopping to do."

"Not Dad. Usually he just calls up the Personal Shopper at Hobson's store and says: 'She's five-feet three, size twelve and likes bright colors. Send out something done up in gift wrapping and charge to my account.'" Penny sighed drearily. "Then after Christmas I have to take it back and ask for an exchange."

"Have you ever tried giving your father a list?" suggested Mrs. Downey, smiling at the description.

"Often. He nearly always ignores it."

"What did you ask him for this year?"

"Only a new automobile."

"Only! My goodness, aren't your tastes rather expensive?"

"Oh, he won't give it to me," replied Penny. "I'll probably get a sweater with pink and blue stripes or some dead merchandise the store couldn't pawn off on anyone except an unsuspecting father."

Mrs. Downey laughed as she picked up the tray.

"I hope your father will be able to get to Pine Top for Christmas."

"So do I," agreed Penny, frowning. "I thought when I wired him that Harvey Maxwell was here he would come right away."

"He may have decided it would do no good to contact the man. Knowing Mr. Maxwell I doubt if your father could make any sort of deal with him."

"If only he would come here he might be able to learn something which would help his case," Penny declared earnestly. "Maxwell and Fergus are mixed up in some queer business."

Mrs. Downey smiled tolerantly. While she always listened attentively to Penny's theories and observations, she had not been greatly excited by her tale of the mysterious Green Room. She knew the two men were unscrupulous in a business way and that they were making every effort to force her to give up the lodge, but she could not bring herself to believe they were involved in more serious affairs. She thought that Penny's great eagerness to prove Harvey Maxwell's dishonesty had caused her imagination to run riot.

"Francine Sellberg wouldn't be at Pine Top if something weren't in the wind," Penny went on reflectively. "She followed Ralph Fergus and Maxwell here. And that in itself was rather strange."

"How do you mean, Penny?"

"Fergus must have been having trouble in managing the hotel or he wouldn't have gone to Riverview to see Maxwell. What he had to say evidently couldn't be trusted to a letter or a telegram."

"Mr. Fergus often absents himself on trips. Now and then he goes to Canada."

"I wonder why?" asked Penny alertly.

"He and Mr. Maxwell have a hotel there, I've heard. I doubt if his trips have any particular significance."

"Well, at any rate, Fergus brought Maxwell back from Riverview to help him solve some weighty problem. From their talk on the plane, I gathered they were plotting to put you out of business, Mrs. Downey."

"I think you are right there, Penny."

"But why should your lodge annoy them? You could never take a large number of guests away from their hotel."

"Ralph Fergus is trying to buy up the entire mountainside," Mrs. Downey declared bitterly. "He purchased the site of the old mine, and I can't see what good it will ever do the hotel."

"You don't suppose there's valuable mineral—"

"No," Mrs. Downey broke in with an amused laugh. "The mine played out years ago."

"Has Mr. Fergus tried to buy your lodge?"

"He's made me two different offers. Both were hardly worth considering. If he comes through with any reasonable proposition I may sell. My future plans depend a great deal upon whether or not Peter Jasko is willing to renew a lease on the ski slopes."

"When does the lease expire, Mrs. Downey?"

"The end of next month. I've asked Mr. Jasko to come and see me as soon as he can. However, I have almost no hope he'll sign a new lease."

Mrs. Downey carried the tray to the door. There she paused to inquire: "Anything I can bring you, Penny? A book or a magazine?"

"No, thank you. But you might give me my portable typewriter. I think I'll write a letter to Dad just to remind him he still has a daughter."

Pulling a table to the bedside, Mrs. Downey placed the typewriter and paper on it before going away. Penny propped herself up with pillows and rolled a blank sheet into the machine.

At the top of the page she pecked out: "Bulletin." After the dateline, she began in her best journalistic style, using upper case letters:

"PENNY PARKER, ATTRACTIVE AND TALENTED DAUGHTER OF ANTHONY PARKER, WHILE RIDING THE TAIL OF A RACING BOB-SLED WAS THROWN FOR A TEN YARD LOSS, SUSTAINING NUMEROUS BRUISES. THE PATIENT IS BEARING HER SUFFERING WITH FORTITUDE AND ANTICIPATES BEING IN CIRCULATION BY GLMLFFLS"

Penny stared at the last word she had written. Inadvertently, her fingers had struck the wrong letters. She had intended to write "tomorrow." With an exclamation of impatience she jerked the paper from the machine.

And then she studied the sentence she had typed with new interest. There was something strangely familiar about the jumbled word, GLMLFFLS.

"It looks a little like that coded message I found!" she thought excitedly.

Forgetting her bruises, Penny rolled out of bed. She struck the floor with a moan of anguish. Hobbling over to the dresser, she found the scrap of paper which she had saved, and brought it back to the bed.

The third word in the message was similar, although not the same as the one she had written by accident. Penny typed them one above the other.

GLMLFFLS

GLULFFLS

"They're identical except for the third letter," she mused. "Why, I believe I have it! You simply strike the letter directly below the true one—that is, the one in the next row of keys. And when your true letter is in the bottom row, you strike the corresponding key on the top row. That's why I wrote an M for a U!"

Penny was certain she had deciphered the third word of the code and that it was the same as she had written unintentionally. Quickly she wrote out the entire jumbled message, and under it her translation.

YL GFZKY GLULFFLS

NO TRAIN TOMORROW

"That's it!" she chortled, bounding up and down in bed.

And then her elation fled away. A puzzled expression settled over her face.

"I have it, only I haven't," she muttered. "What can the message mean? There are no trains at Pine Top—not even a railroad station. This leaves everything in a worse puzzle than before!"

***

CHAPTER 17

STRANGE SOUNDS

Penny felt reasonably certain that she had deciphered the code correctly, but although she studied over the message for nearly an hour, she could make nothing of it.

"No train tomorrow," she repeated to herself. "How silly! Perhaps it means, no *plane* tomorrow."

She worked out the code a second time, checking her letters carefully. There was no mistake.

Later in the evening when Mrs. Downey stopped to inquire how she was feeling, Penny asked her about the train service near Pine Top.

"The nearest railroad is thirty miles away," replied the woman. "It is a very tedious journey to Pine Top unless one comes by airplane."

"Is the plane service under the control of the Fergus-Maxwell interests?"

"Not to my knowledge," returned Mrs. Downey, surprised by the question. "This same airline company sent planes here even before the Fergus hotel was built, but not on a regular schedule."

Left alone once more, Penny slipped the typewritten message under her pillow and drew a long sigh. Somehow she was making no progress in any line. From whom had Ralph Fergus received the coded note, and what was its meaning?

"I'll never learn anything lying here in bed," she murmured gloomily. "Tomorrow I'll get up even if it kills me."

True to her resolve, she was downstairs in time for breakfast the next morning.

"Oh, Penny," protested Mrs. Downey anxiously, "don't you think you should have stayed in bed? I can tell it hurts you to walk."

"I'll limber up with exercise. I may take a little hike down to the village later on."

Mrs. Downey sadly shook her head. She thought that Penny had entirely too much determination for her own good.

Until ten o'clock Penny remained at the lodge, rather hoping that Sara Jasko would put in an appearance. When it was evident that the girl was not coming, she bundled herself into warm clothing and walked painfully down the mountain road. Observing old Peter Jasko in the yard near the cabin, she did not pause but went on until she drew near the Fergus hotel.

"I wish I dared go in there," she thought, stopping to rest for a moment. "But I most certainly would be chased out."

Penny sat down on a log bench in plain view of the hostelry. Forming a snowball, she tossed it at a squirrel. The animal scurried quickly to a low-hanging tree branch and chattered his violent disapproval.

"Brother, that's the way I feel, too," declared Penny soberly. "You express my sentiments perfectly."

She was still sunk in deep gloom when she heard a light step behind her. Turning her head stiffly she saw Maxine Miller tramping through the snow toward her.

"If it isn't Miss Parker!" the actress exclaimed with affected enthusiasm. "How delighted I am to see you again, my dear. I heard about the marvelous way you stopped the bob-sled yesterday. Such courage! You deserve a medal."

"I would rather have some new skin," said Penny.

"I imagine you do feel rather bruised and battered," the actress replied with a show of sympathy. "But how proud you must be of yourself! Everyone is talking about it! As I was telling Mr. Jasko last night—"

"You were talking with Peter Jasko?" broke in Penny.

"Yes, he came to the hotel to see Mr. Fergus—something about a lease, I think. Imagine! He hadn't heard a word about the accident, and his granddaughter was in it!"

"You told him all about it I suppose?" Penny asked with a moan.

"Yes, he was tremendously impressed. Why, what is the matter? Do you have a pain somewhere?"

"Several of them," said Penny. "Go on. What did Mr. Jasko say?"

"Not much of anything. He just listened. Shouldn't I have told him?"

"I am sorry you did, but it can't be helped now. Mr. Jasko doesn't like to have his granddaughter ski or take any part in winter sports."

"Oh, I didn't know that. Then I did let the cat out of the bag. I thought he acted rather peculiar."

"He was bound to have found out about it sooner or later," Penny sighed. With a quick change of mood she inquired: "What's doing down at the hotel? Any excitement?"

"Everything is about as usual. I've sold two fur coats. Don't you think you might be interested in one yourself?"

"I would be interested but my pocketbook wouldn't."

"These coats are a marvelous bargain," Miss Miller declared. "Why don't you at least look at them and try one on. Come down to the hotel with me now and I'll arrange for you to meet my employer."

"Well—" Penny hesitated, "could we enter the hotel by the back way?"

"I suppose so," replied the actress in surprise. "You're sensitive about being crippled?"

"That's right. I don't care to meet anyone I know."

"We can slip into the hotel the back way, then. Very few persons use the rear corridors."

Penny and Miss Miller approached the building without being observed. They entered at the back, meeting neither Ralph Fergus or Harvey Maxwell.

"Can you climb a flight of stairs?" the actress asked doubtfully.

"Oh, yes, easily. I much prefer it to the elevator."

"You really walk with only a slight limp," declared Miss Miller. "I see no reason why you should feel so sensitive."

"It's just my nature," laughed Penny. "Lend me your arm, and up we go."

They ascended to the second floor. Miss Miller motioned for the girl to sit down on a sofa not far from the elevator.

"You wait here and I'll bring my employer," she offered. "I'll be back in a few minutes."

"Who is this man?" inquired Penny.

The actress did not hear the question. She had turned away and was descending the stairs again to the lobby floor.

For a moment or two the girl sat with her head against the back rest of the sofa, completely relaxed. The trip down the mountainside had tired her more than she had expected. She was afraid she had made a mistake in coming boldly to the hotel. If Harvey Maxwell caught her there he would not treat her kindly.

As for seeing the fur coats, she had no intention of ever making a purchase. She had agreed to look at them because she was curious to learn the identity of Miss Miller's employer, as well as the nature of the proposition which might be made her.

Presently, Penny's attention was directed to a distant sound, low and rhythmical, carrying a staccato overtone.

At first the girl paid little heed to the sound. No doubt it was just another noise incidental to a large hotel—some machine connected with the cleaning services perhaps.

But gradually, the sound impressed itself deeper on her mind. There was something strangely familiar about it, yet she could not make a positive identification.

Penny arose from the sofa and listened intently. The sound seemed to be coming from far down the left hand hall. She proceeded slowly, pausing frequently in an effort to discover whence it came. She entered a side hall and the noise increased noticeably.

Suddenly Penny heard footsteps behind her. Turning slightly she was dismayed to see Ralph Fergus coming toward her. For an instant she was certain he meant to eject her from the hotel. Then, she realized that his head was down, and that he was paying no particular attention to her.

Penny kept her back turned and walked even more slowly. The man overtook her, passed without so much as bestowing a glance upon her. He went to a door which bore the number 27 and, taking a key from his pocket, fitted it into the lock.

Penny would have thought nothing of his act, save that as he swung back the door, the strange sound which previously had drawn her attention, increased in volume. It died away again as the door closed behind Fergus.

Waiting a moment, Penny went on down the hall and paused near the room where the hotel man had entered. She looked quickly up and down the hall. No one was in sight.

Moving closer, she pressed her ear to the panel. There was no sound inside the room, but as she waited, the rhythmical chugging began again. And suddenly she knew what caused it—a teletype machine!

Often in her father's newspaper office Penny had heard that same sound and had watched the printers recording news from all parts of the country. There was no mistaking it, for she could plainly distinguish the clicking of the type against the platen, the low hum of the machine itself, the quick clang of the little bell at the end of each line of copy.

"What would the hotel be doing with a teletype?" she mused. "They print no newspapers here."

Into Penny's mind leaped a startling thought. The coded message in upper case letters which Fergus had dropped in the snow! Might it not have been printed by a teletype machine?

"But what significance *could* it have?" she asked herself. "From what office are the messages being sent and for what purpose?"

It seemed to Penny that the answer to her many questions might lie, not in the Green Room as she had supposed, but close at hand in Number 27.

Her ear pressed to the panel, the girl made out a low rumble of voices above the clatter of the teletype. Ralph Fergus was talking with another man but she could not distinguish a word they were saying. So intent was she that she failed to hear a step behind her.

A mop handle clattered to the floor, making a loud sound on the tiles. Penny whirled about in confusion. A cleaning maid stood beside her, regarding her with evident though unspoken suspicion.

***

CHAPTER 18

QUESTIONS AND CLUES

"**G**ood morning," stammered Penny, backing from the door. "Were you wanting to get into this room?"

"No, I never clean in there," answered the maid, still watching the girl with suspicion. "You're looking for someone?"

Penny knew that she had been observed listening at the door. It would be foolish to pretend otherwise.

She answered frankly: "No, I was passing through the corridor when I heard a strange sound in this room. Do you hear it?"

The maid nodded and her distrustful attitude changed to one of indifference.

"It's a machine of some sort," she answered. "I hear it running every once in a while."

Penny was afraid to loiter by the door any longer lest her own voice bring Ralph Fergus to investigate. As the cleaning woman picked up her mop and started on down the hall, she fell into step with her.

"Who occupies Room 27?" she inquired casually.

"No one," said the maid. "The hotel uses it."

"What goes on in there anyway? I thought I heard teletype machines."

The maid was unfamiliar with the technical name Penny had used. "It's just a contraption that prints letters and figures," she informed. "When I first came to work at the hotel I made a mistake and went in there to do some cleaning. Mr. Fergus, he didn't like it and said I wasn't to bother to dust up there again."

"Doesn't anyone go into the room except Mr. Fergus?"

"Just him and George Jewitt."

"And who is he? One of the owners of the hotel?"

"Oh, no. George Jewitt works for Mr. Fergus. He takes care of the machines, I guess."

"You were saying that the machine prints letters and figures," prompted Penny. "Do you mean messages one can read?"

"It was writing crazy-like when I watched it. The letters didn't make sense nohow. Mr. Fergus he told me the machines were being used in some experiment the hotel was carrying on."

"Who occupies the nearby rooms?" Penny questioned. "I should think they would be disturbed by the machines."

"Rooms on this corridor are never assigned unless everything else is full up," the maid explained.

Pausing at a door, the cleaning woman fitted a master key into the lock.

"There's one thing more I'm rather curious about," said Penny quickly. "It's this Green Room I hear folks mentioning."

The maid gazed at her suspiciously again. "I don't know anything about any Green Room," she replied.

Entering the bedroom with her cleaning paraphernalia, she closed the door behind her.

"Went a bit too far that time," thought Penny, "but at least I learned a few facts of interest."

Turning, she retraced her steps to Room 27, but she was afraid to linger there lest Ralph Fergus should discover her loitering in the hall. Miss Miller had not put in an appearance when she returned to the elevators. She decided not to wait.

Scribbling a brief note of explanation, Penny left the paper in a corner of the sofa and hobbled down the stairway to the first floor. She let herself out the back way without attracting undue attention. Safely in the open once more she retreated to her bench under the ice-coated trees.

"I need to give this whole problem a good think," she told herself. "Here I have a number of perfectly good clues but they don't fit together. I'm almost as far from getting evidence against Fergus and Maxwell as I was at the start."

Penny could not understand why the hotel would have need for teletype machine service. Such machines were used in newspaper offices, for railroad communication, brokerage service, and occasionally in very large plants with widely separated branch offices. Suddenly she recalled that her father had once told her Mr. Maxwell kept in touch with his chain of hotels by means of such a wire service. Surely it was an expensive and unnecessary means of communication.

The cleaning woman's information that messages came through in unintelligible form convinced Penny a code was being used—a code to which she had the key. But why did Maxwell and Fergus find it necessary to employ one? If their messages concerned only the routine operation of the various hotels in the chain, there would be no need for secrecy.

The one message she had interpreted—"No Train Tomorrow"— undoubtedly had been received by teletype transmission. But Penny could not hazard a guess as to its true meaning. She feared it might be in double code, and that the words did not have the significance usually attributed to them.

"If only I could get into Room 27 and get my hands on additional code messages I might be able to make something out of it," she mused. "The problem is how to do it without being caught."

Penny had not lost interest in the Green Room. She was inclined to believe that its mystery was closely associated with the communication system of the hotel. But since, for the time being at least, the problem of penetrating beyond the guarded Green Door seemed unsolvable, she thought it wiser to center her sleuthing attack elsewhere.

"All I can do for the next day or so is to keep an eye on Ralph Fergus and Harvey Maxwell," she told herself. "If I see a chance to get inside Room 27 I'll take it."

Penny arose with a sigh. She would not be likely to have such a chance unless she made it for herself. And in her present battered state, her mind somehow refused to invent clever schemes.

The walk back up the mountain road was a long and tiring one. Finally reaching the lodge after many pauses for rest, Penny stood for a time watching the skiers, and then entered the house.

Mrs. Downey was not in the kitchen. Hearing voices from the living room, Penny went to the doorway and paused there. The hotel woman was talking with a visitor, old Peter Jasko.

"Oh, I'm sorry," Penny apologized for her intrusion. She started to retreat.

Peter Jasko saw her and the muscles of his leathery face tightened. Pushing back his chair he got quickly to his feet.

"You're the one who has been trespassing on my land!" he accused, his voice unsteady from anger. "You've been helping my granddaughter disobey my orders!"

Taken by surprise, Penny could think of nothing to say in her own defense.

After his first outburst, Peter Jasko ignored the girl. Turning once more to Mrs. Downey he said in a rasping voice:

"You have my final decision, Ma'am. I shall not renew the lease."

"Please, Mr. Jasko," Mrs. Downey argued quietly. "Think what this means to me! If I lose the ski slopes I shall be compelled to give up the lodge. I've already offered you more than I can afford to pay."

"Money ain't no object," the old man retorted. "I'm against the whole proposition."

"Nothing I can say will make you reconsider?"

"Nothing, Ma'am."

Picking up his cap, a ridiculous looking affair with ear muffs, Peter Jasko brushed past Penny and went out the door.

***

CHAPTER 19

PETER JASKO SERVES NOTICE

After the old man had gone, Penny spoke apologetically to Mrs. Downey.

"Oh, I'm so sorry! I ruined everything, coming in just when I did."

Mrs. Downey sat with her hands folded in her lap, staring out the window after the retreating figure of Peter Jasko.

"No, it wasn't your fault, Penny."

"He was angry at me because I've been helping Sara get in and out of the cabin. I never should have done it."

"Perhaps not," agreed Mrs. Downey, "but it would have made no difference in regard to the lease. I've been expecting Jasko's decision. Even so, it comes as a blow. This last week I had been turning ideas over in my mind, trying to think of a way I could keep on here. Now everything is settled."

Penny crossed the room and slipped an arm about the woman's shoulders.

"I'm as sorry as I can be."

With a sudden change of mood, Mrs. Downey arose and gave Penny's hand an affectionate squeeze.

"Losing the lodge won't mean the end of the world," she said lightly. "While I may not be able to sell the place for a very good price now that the ski slopes are gone, I'll at least get something from Mr. Maxwell. And I have a small income derived from my husband's insurance policy."

"Where will you go if you leave here?"

"I haven't given that part any thought," admitted Mrs. Downey. "I may do a little traveling. I have a sister in Texas I might visit."

"You'll be lonesome for Pine Top."

"Yes," admitted Mrs. Downey, "this place will always seem like home to me. And I've lived a busy, useful life for so many years it will be hard to let go."

"Possibly Peter Jasko will reconsider his decision."

Mrs. Downey smiled and shook her head. "Not Peter. I've known him for many years, although I can't say I ever became acquainted with him. Once he makes a stand nothing can sway him."

"Is he entirely right in his mind?" Penny asked dubiously.

"Oh, yes. He's peculiar, that's all. And he's getting old."

Despite Mrs. Downey's avowal that no one was responsible for Peter Jasko's decision, Penny considered herself at fault. She could not blame the old man for being provoked because she had helped his granddaughter escape from the cabin.

"If I went down there and apologized it might do some good," she thought. "At least, nothing will be lost by trying."

Penny turned the plan over in her mind, saying nothing about it to Mrs. Downey. It seemed to her that the best way would be to wait for a few hours until Peter Jasko had been given an opportunity to get over his anger.

The afternoon dragged on slowly. Toward nightfall, finding confinement intolerable, Penny ventured out-of-doors to try her skis. She was thrilled to discover that she could use them without too much discomfort.

Going to the kitchen window, she called to Mrs. Downey that she intended to do a little skiing and might be late for dinner.

"Oh, Penny, you're not able," the woman protested, raising the sash. "It's only your determination which drives you on."

"I'm feeling much better," insisted Penny. "I want to go down the mountain and see Sara."

"It will be a hard climb back," warned Mrs. Downey. "And the radio reported another bad storm coming."

"That's why I want to go now," answered Penny. "We may be snowbound by tomorrow."

"Well, if you must go, don't overtax your strength," cautioned Mrs. Downey.

Penny wrapped a woolen scarf tightly about her neck as a protection against the biting wind. Cautiously, she skied down the trail, finding its frozen surface treacherous, and scarcely familiar. In the rapidly gathering dusk nothing looked exactly the same as by daylight. Trees towered like unfriendly giants, obscuring the path.

Before Penny had covered half the distance to Jasko's cabin, snowflakes, soft and damp, began to fall. They came faster and faster, the wind whirling them directly into her face. She kept her head down and wished that she had remained by the crackling log fire at the Downey lodge.

Swinging out of the forest, Penny was hard pressed to remember the trail. As she hesitated, trying to decide which way to go, she felt her skis slipping along a downgrade where none should have been. Too late, she realized that she was heading down into a deep ravine which terminated in an ice-sheeted river below.

Throwing herself flat, Penny sought to save herself, but she kept sliding, sliding. A stubby evergreen at last stayed her fall. She clung helplessly to it for a moment, recovering her breath. Then she tried to pull herself up the steep incline. She slipped and barely caught hold of the bush to save herself from another bad fall. Sharp pains shot through her side.

"Now I've fixed myself for sure," she thought. "How will I ever get out of this hole?"

The ravine offered protection from the chill wind, but the snow was sifting down steadily. Penny could feel her clothing becoming thoroughly soaked. If she should lie still she soon would freeze.

   Behind the Green Door

Again Penny tried to struggle up the bank, and again she slid backwards. From sheer desperation rather than because she cherished a hope that anyone would hear, Penny shouted for help.

An answering halloo echoed to her through the trees.

Penny dared not hope that the voice was other than her own. "Help! Help!" she called once more.

Her heart leaped. The cry which came back definitely belonged to a man! And as she marveled at the miracle of a rescue, a dark figure loomed up at the rim of the ravine.

A gruff voice called to her: "Hold on! Don't try to move! I'll get a rope and be back!"

The man faded back into the darkness. Penny clung to the bush until it seemed her arms would break. Snow fell steadily, caking her hood and penetrating the woolen suit.

Then as the girl lost all awareness of time, she caught the flash of a lighted lantern. Her rescuer appeared again at the top of the ravine and lowered a rope. She grasped it, wrapping it tightly about her wrist, and climbed as best she could while the man pulled from above.

At last Penny reached the top, falling in an exhausted heap on the snow. Raising her head she stared into the face of her rescuer. The man was Peter Jasko.

He recognized her at the same instant.

"You!" he exclaimed.

For one disturbing moment Penny thought the old man meant to push her back down into the yawning ravine. In the yellow glow of the lantern, the expression of his face was terrifying.

Gaining control of himself, Peter Jasko demanded gruffly: "Hurt?"

"I've twisted my ankle." Penny pulled herself up from the ground, took a step, and recoiled with pain.

"Let me have a look at it."

Jasko bent down and examined the ankle.

"No bones broken," he said. "You're luckier than you deserve. Any fool who doesn't know enough to keep off skis ought to be crippled for life!"

"Such a cheerful philosophy," observed Penny ironically. "Well, thanks anyhow for saving me. Even if you are sorry you did it."

The old man made no immediate reply. He stood gazing down at Penny.

"Reckon I owe you something," he said grudgingly. "Sara told me how you kept the bob-sled from going off the track. Injured yourself, too, didn't you?"

"Yes."

"You had no business helping Sara go against my will," the old man said, his anger rising again. "I told you to stay away, didn't I?"

"You did. I was sorry to disobey your orders, Mr. Jasko, but I think you are unjust to your granddaughter."

"You do, eh?"

"And you're not being fair to Mrs. Downey either," Penny went on courageously. "She's struggled for years to make her lodge profitable, fought against overwhelming odds while the Fergus interests have done everything they can to put her out of business. Unless you renew her lease, she'll be forced to leave Pine Top."

"So?" inquired the old man, unmoved.

"She's fighting with her back to the wall. And now you've dealt her the final blow."

"No one asked Mrs. Downey to come here in the first place," replied Peter Jasko. "Or them other hotel people either. Pine Top can get along without the lot of 'em. The sooner they all clear out the better I'll like it."

"I'm sure of that," said Penny. "You don't care how much trouble you cause other folks. Because of your own son's death you have taken an unnatural attitude toward skiing. You hate everything remotely connected with the sport. But it isn't fair. Your granddaughter has a right to a certain amount of freedom."

Peter Jasko listened to the girl's words in silence. When she had finished he said in a strangely shaken voice:

"My son met his death going on ten years ago. It was on this trail—"

"I'm sorry," Penny said contritely. "I shouldn't have spoken the way I did. Actually, I was on my way down the mountain to tell you I deeply regret helping Sara to go against your will."

"My granddaughter is headstrong," the old man replied slowly. "I want what's best for her. That's why I've tried to protect her."

"I'm sure you've done what you thought was right," Penny returned. "Why don't you see Mrs. Downey again and—"

"No!" said the old man stubbornly. "You can't say anything which will make me change my mind. Take my arm and see if you can walk!"

Penny struggled forward, supported by Jasko's strong arm. Although each step sent a wracking pain through her leg she made no sound of protest.

"You can't make it that way," the old man declared, pausing. "I'll have to fix up a sled and pull you."

Going back for Penny's skis which had been left at the top of the ravine, he lashed them together. She lay full length on the runners, and he towed her until they came within view of the cabin. A light glowed in the window.

On level ground, Penny tried walking again, and managed to reach the cabin door.

"You go on inside," the old man directed. "I'll hitch up the bob-sled and take you home."

Penny pushed open the door only to hesitate on the threshold. The room was filled with tobacco smoke. Two men sat at the table, and directly behind them stood Sara Jasko.

The girl came swiftly to the door. She gave Penny a warm smile of welcome, not noticing that she had been hurt, and said anxiously to Mr. Jasko:

"Grandfather, you have visitors. Mr. Fergus and Mr. Maxwell are waiting to see you. I think it's about the lease."

"I've nothing to say to them," returned the old man grimly.

Nevertheless, he followed the two girls into the room, closing the door against the wind and snow.

The situation was an awkward one for Penny. Ralph Fergus and Harvey Maxwell both stared at her with undisguised dislike and suspicion. Then, the former arose, and ignoring her entirely, stepped forward to meet the old man, his hand extended.

"Good evening, sir," he said affably. "Mr. Maxwell and I have a little business to discuss with you, if you can spare us a moment."

Peter Jasko ignored the offered hand.

"I haven't changed my mind since the last time we talked," he said. "I'm not signing any lease!"

Penny scarcely heard the words for she was staring beyond Ralph Fergus at his overcoat which hung over the vacated chair. The garment was light brown and the top button, a large one of the same color, had been torn from the cloth.

Shifting her gaze, Penny glanced at Sara. The girl nodded her head slowly up and down. She, too, had made the important observation, and was thinking the same thought. There could be little doubt of it—Ralph Fergus was the man who had weakened the brake rod of their bob-sled!

***

CHAPTER 20

VISITORS

"May we see you alone, Mr. Jasko?" requested Ralph Fergus. "I don't reckon there's any need for being so all-fired private," the old man retorted, his hand on the doorknob. "If you want to talk with me speak your piece right out. I got to hitch up the team."

Mr. Fergus and his companion, Harvey Maxwell, glanced coldly toward Penny who had sunk down into a chair and was massaging her ankle. They were reluctant to reveal their business before her but there was no other way.

"We can't talk with you very well while you're poised for flight, Mr. Jasko," Ralph Fergus said placatingly. "My friend, Maxwell, has prepared a paper which he would like to have you look over."

"I'm not signin' anything!"

"Good for you, Grandfather!" muttered Sara under her breath.

The two men pretended not to hear. Mr. Maxwell took a folded document from his pocket and spread it out on the kitchen table.

"Will you just read this, please, Mr. Jasko? You'll find our terms are more than generous."

"I ain't interested in your terms," he snapped. "I'm aimin' to keep every acre of my land."

"We're not asking you to sell, only to lease," Mr. Fergus interposed smoothly. "Now we understand that your deal with Mrs. Downey has fallen through, so there's no reason why you shouldn't lease the ski slopes to us. We are prepared to offer you twice the amount she proposed to give you."

Mr. Jasko stubbornly shook his head.

"You're taking a very short-sighted attitude," said Ralph Fergus, beginning to lose patience. "At least read the paper."

"No."

"Think what this would mean to your granddaughter," interposed Harvey Maxwell. "Pretty clothes, school in the city perhaps—"

"Don't listen to them, Grandfather," spoke Sara quickly. "I have enough clothes. And Pine Top school suits me."

"You're wastin' your time and mine," said Peter Jasko. "I ain't leasing my land to anybody."

"We're only asking you to sign a three-year lease—" Mr. Fergus argued.

"Can't you understand plain language?" the old man cried. "You think money will buy everything, but you got another guess coming. I've seen enough skiing at Pine Top and I aim to put a stop to it!"

"It's no use," said Harvey Maxwell resignedly to his companion.

Ralph Fergus picked up the paper and thrust it into his overcoat pocket. "You're an old fool, Jasko!" he muttered.

"Don't you dare speak that way to my grandfather!" Sara cried, her eyes stormy. "You had your nerve coming here anyway, after that trick you tried!"

"Trick?"

"You deliberately weakened the brake rod of our bob-sled."

Ralph Fergus laughed in the girl's face. "You're as touched as your grandfather," he said.

"Perhaps you can explain what became of the top button of your overcoat," suggested Penny coming to Sara's support. "And don't try to tell us it's home in your sewing basket!"

                                                    Behind the Green Door

Ralph Fergus' hand groped at the vacant spot on his coat.

"What does a button have to do with the bob-sled accident?" inquired Harvey Maxwell.

"It happens that we found a large brown button in the tool house at the Downey lodge," replied Penny. "Also a little additional evidence which rather suggests Mr. Fergus is the one who tampered with the bob-sled."

"Ridiculous!" protested the hotel man. "I've not even been near Mrs. Downey's lodge in weeks."

"I know that's a lie," said Peter Jasko. "I saw you goin' up that way Friday night."

"And you went there to damage the bob-sled!" Sara accused. "You didn't care how many persons might be injured in an accident!"

Ralph Fergus' face was an angry red. "What reason would I have for doing anything like that?" he demanded.

"Guests were being drawn from your hotel because bob-sledding was increasing in popularity," said Penny quietly. "Nothing would please you more than to put Mrs. Downey out of business."

"Aren't you drawing rather sweeping conclusions?" inquired Harvey Maxwell in an insolent tone. "A button isn't very certain evidence. So many persons wear buttons, you know."

"I lost this one from my coat weeks ago," added Ralph Fergus.

"It was your button we found," Sara accused.

Peter Jasko had been listening intently to the argument, taking little part in it. But now, with a quick movement which belied his age, he moved across the kitchen toward the gun rack on the wall.

"Let's be getting out of here," muttered Harvey Maxwell.

He and Ralph Fergus both bolted out of the door. Their sudden flight delighted Sara who broke into a fit of laughter.

"Why don't you shoot once or twice into the air just to give 'em a good fright?" she asked her grandfather.

The old man, shotgun in hand, had followed the two men to the door. But he did not shoot.

"Grandfather wouldn't hurt a flea really," chuckled Sara. "At least, not unless it was trying to make him sign something."

"Ralph Fergus acted guilty, all right," declared Penny, bending down to massage her injured ankle. "But it may have been a mistake for us to accuse him."

"I couldn't help it," answered Sara. "When I saw that button missing from his coat, I had to say something about it."

Peter Jasko put away his shotgun, turning once more to the door. "I'll hitch up the team," he said. "Sara, get some liniment and see what you can do for Miss Parker's ankle."

"Your ankle?" gasped Sara, staring at Penny. "Have you hurt yourself again?"

"I managed to fall into the ravine a few minutes ago. Your grandfather saved me."

Sara darted to the stove to get a pan of warm water. She stripped off Penny's woolen stockings and examined the foot as she soaked it.

"I suppose this will put me on the shelf for another day or so," Penny observed gloomily. "But I'm lucky I didn't break my neck."

"The ankle is swollen," Sara said, "I'll wrap it with a bandage and that may make it feel better."

With a practiced hand she wound strips of gauze and adhesive tape about the ankle.

"There, how does it feel now?"

"Much better," said Penny. "Thanks a lot. I—I feel rather mean to put your grandfather to so much trouble, especially after the way I've crossed him."

"Oh, don't you worry about Grandfather," laughed Sara. "He likes you, Penny."

"He *likes* me?"

"I could tell by the way he acted tonight. He respects a person who stands up to him."

"I said some rather unnecessary things," Penny declared regretfully. "I was provoked because he wouldn't sign a lease with Mrs. Downey. After hearing what he said to Fergus and Maxwell I realize nothing will sway him."

Sara sighed as she helped her friend put on her shoe again.

"I'm afraid not. I'll do what I can to influence him, but I can tell you now he'll never listen to me. Grandfather is just the way he is, and one can't budge him an inch."

Peter Jasko soon had the team hitched to the bob-sled. He and Sara helped Penny in, wrapping blankets around her so that she would be snug and warm during the ride up the mountain.

"Come down again whenever you can," invited Sara. "Only the next time don't try it after dark if you're on skis."

Penny glanced at the old man, but his face showed no displeasure. Apparently, he no longer regarded her as an interloper.

"I'll come as soon as I can," she replied.

Peter Jasko clucked to the horses, and the sled moved away from the cabin. Sara stood in the doorway until it was out of sight.

During the slow ride up the mountain side, the old man did not speak. But as they came at last to the Downey lodge, and he lifted her from the sled, he actually smiled.

"I reckon it won't do any good to lock Sara up after this," he said. "You're both too smart for an old codger like me."

"Thank you, Mr. Jasko," answered Penny, her eyes shining. "Thank you for everything."

The door of the lodge had opened, and Mrs. Downey, a coat thrown over her shoulders, hurried out into the snow. Not wishing to be drawn into a conversation, Jasko leaped back into the sled, and with a curt, "Good evening," drove away.

With Mrs. Downey's help, Penny hobbled into the house, and there related her latest misadventure.

"I declare, you'll be in the hospital yet," sighed the woman. "I feel tempted to adopt Mr. Jasko's tactics and lock you up in your room."

"I'll stay there without being locked in," declared Penny. "I've had enough skiing to last me until Christmas at least."

In the morning she felt so stiff and battered that she could barely get out of bed. However, her ankle was somewhat better and when occasion demanded, she could hobble across the room without support.

"You ought to be all right in a day or so if only you'll stay off your foot and give it a chance to get well," declared Mrs. Downey.

"It's hard to sit still," sighed Penny. "There are so many things I ought to be doing."

From the kitchen window she could see the Fergus hotel far down in the valley. She was impatient to pay another visit there, although she realized that after the previous evening's encounter with Ralph Fergus and Harvey Maxwell, it would be more difficult than ever to gain admittance.

"Somehow I must manage to get into Room 27 and learn what is going on there," she thought. "But how? That is the question!"

Ever an active, energetic person, Penny became increasingly restless as the day dragged on. During mid-afternoon, observing that Jake had hitched up the team to the sled, she inquired if he were driving down to Pine Top.

"Yes, I am sending him after supplies," explained Mrs. Downey. "And the newspapers—if there are any."

"I wish I could go along for the ride."

Mrs. Downey regarded Penny skeptically.

"Oh, I wouldn't get out of the sled," Penny said.

"Is that a promise?"

"I'll make it one. Nothing less than a fire or an earthquake will get me out."

Jake brought the sled to the door, and helped the girl into it. The day was cold. Snow fell steadily. Mrs. Downey tucked warm bricks at Penny's feet and wrapped her snugly in woolen blankets.

The ride down the mountainside was without event. Penny began to regret that she had made the trip, for the weather was more unpleasant than she had anticipated. She burrowed deeper and deeper into the blankets.

Jake pulled up at a hitching post in front of Pine Top's grocery store.

"It won't take me long," he said.

Penny climbed down in the bottom of the sled, rearranging her blankets so that only her eyes and forehead were exposed to the cold. She had been sitting there for some minutes when her attention was drawn to a man who was approaching from far down the street. Recognizing him as Ralph Fergus, she watched with interest.

At the drugstore he paused. As if by prearrangement, Benny Smith came out of the building. Penny was too far away to hear their exchange of words, but she saw the boy give all of his newspapers to Ralph Fergus. In return, he received a bill which she guessed might be of fairly high denomination.

"Probably five dollars," she thought. "The boy sells all his papers to Fergus because he can make more that way than by peddling them one by one. And he's paid to keep quiet about it."

Penny was not especially surprised to discover that the hotel man was buying up all the papers, for she had suspected he was behind the trick.

"There's no law against it," she told herself. "That's the trouble. Fergus and Maxwell are clever. So far they've done nothing which could possibly get them into legal trouble."

Presently Jake came out of the grocery store, carrying a large box of supplies which he stowed in the sled.

"I'll get the papers and then we'll be ready to start."

"Don't bother," said Penny. "There aren't any. I just saw Ralph Fergus buy them all from the boy."

"Fergus, eh? And he's been puttin' it out that the papers never caught the plane!"

"It was just another one of his little tricks to make Mrs. Downey's guests dissatisfied."

"Now we know what he's about we'll put a stop to it!"

"Yes," agreed Penny, "but he'll only think of something new to try."

As they started back toward the Downey lodge, she was quiet, turning over various matters in her mind. Since Mrs. Downey had decided to sell her business, it scarcely seemed to matter what Ralph Fergus did.

The sled drew near the Jasko cabin and passed it, turning a bend in the road. Suddenly Penny thought she heard her name called. Glancing back she was startled to see Sara Jasko running after the sled.

"Wait, Jake!" Penny commanded. "It's Sara! Something seems to be wrong!"

***

CHAPTER 21

OLD PETER'S DISAPPEARANCE

"Whoa!" shouted Jake, pulling on the reins.

The horses brought the heavy sled to a halt at the side of the road. Sara, breathless from running so fast, hurried up.

"I'm worried about Grandfather," she gasped out.

"He isn't sick?" Penny asked quickly,

"No, but I haven't seen him since early this morning. He went to chop wood at Hatter's place up the mountain. He expected to be back in time for lunch but he hasn't returned."

"He'll likely be along soon," said Jake.

"Oh, you don't know Grandfather," declared Sara, her forehead wrinkling with anxiety. "He always does exactly as he says he will do. He never would have stayed away this long unless something had happened. He's getting on in years and I'm afraid—"

"Jake, couldn't we go up to Hatter's place, wherever it is?" Penny urged.

"Sure. It's not far from Mrs. Downey's."

"Let me ride with you," Sara requested. "I'm sorry to cause you any trouble, but I have a feeling something is wrong."

"Jump in," invited Jake.

Sara climbed into the back of the sled, snuggling down in the blankets beside Penny.

"Grandfather may have hurt himself with the ax," she said uneasily. "Or he could have suffered a stroke. The doctor says he has a touch of heart-trouble, but he never will take care of himself."

"We'll probably find him safe and sound," Penny declared in a comforting way.

Jake stirred the horses to greater activity. In a short while the sled passed the Downey grounds and went on to the Hatter farm. Sara sprang out to unlock the wooden gate which barred entrance to a narrow, private road.

"I see Grandfather's sled!" she exclaimed.

Without waiting for Jake to drive through the gate, she ran on down the road. Hearing her cry of alarm, the man urged his horses on.

Reaching the clearing, Penny and Jake saw Sara gazing about in bewilderment. Peter Jasko's team had been tied to a tree and the sled box was half filled with wood. An ax lay in the deep snow close by. But there was no sign of the old man.

"Where is grandfather?" Sara asked in a dazed voice.

She called his name several times. Hearing no answer, she ran deeper into the woods. Jake leaped from the sled and joined in the search. Penny could not bear to sit helplessly by. Deciding that the emergency was equal to an earthquake or a fire, she eased herself down from the sled.

Steadily falling snow had obliterated all tracks save those made by the new arrivals. There was no clue to indicate whether Peter Jasko had left the scene of his own free will or had been the possible victim of violence.

Jake and Sara searched at the edge of the woods and returned to the clearing to report no success.

"Maybe your granddad went up to Hatter's place to get warm," the man suggested.

"He never would have left his horses without blanketing them," answered Sara. "But let's go there and inquire. Someone may have seen Grandfather."

They drove the bob-sled on through the woods to an unpainted farm house. Claud Hatter himself opened the door, and in response to Sara's anxious question, he told her that he had seen Peter Jasko drive into the place early that morning.

"You didn't see him go away?" Sara asked.

"No, but come to think of it, I noticed a car turn into the road. Must have been about ten o'clock this morning."

"What sort of car?"

The man could give no additional information, for he had not paid particular attention to the automobile. However, he pulled on his heavy coat and boots, offering to help organize a searching party.

Sara and Penny remained at the farm house, but as it became evident that the old man would not be found quickly, Jake returned and took the girls down the mountain to the Downey lodge.

"What could have happened to Grandfather?" Sara repeated over and over. "I can't believe he became dazed and wandered away."

"I wish we knew who came in the car," said Penny. "That might explain a lot."

"You—you think Grandfather met with violence?"

"I hope not," replied Penny earnestly. "But it seems very queer. Did your grandfather have enemies?"

"He antagonizes many folks without meaning to do so. However, I can't think of anyone at Pine Top who could be called an actual enemy."

By nightfall the searching party had grown in size. Nearly every male resident of Pine Top joined in the hunt for Peter Jasko. Even the Fergus hotel sent two employes to help comb the mountainside for the missing old man.

Sara, nearly in a state of collapse, was put to bed by Mrs. Downey, who kept telling the girl over and over that she must not worry. In speaking with Penny, the woman was far from optimistic. She expressed a doubt that Peter Jasko ever would be found alive.

"He may have wandered off and fallen into a crevasse."

"I am inclined to think he may have been spirited away by whoever came up the private road in that car," commented Penny.

"I can't imagine anyone bothering to kidnap Peter Jasko," returned Mrs. Downey. "He has no money."

"It does sound rather fantastic, I admit. Especially in broad daylight. You didn't notice any automobile on the main road this morning did you?"

"Only the Fergus hotel delivery truck. But I was busy. A dozen might have passed without my noticing them."

At nine o'clock Jake came to the lodge with a discouraging report. No trace of Peter Jasko had been found. The search would continue throughout the night.

"Which way are you going?" Penny inquired as the man started to leave the house again. "Up the mountain or down?"

"Down," he returned. "I'm joining a party at Jasko's own place. We aim to start combing the woods on his farm next."

"May I ride with you?" she requested. "I want to go down to the Fergus hotel."

"Penny, your ankle—" protested Mrs. Downey.

"I can get around on it," Penny said hurriedly. "See!" She hobbled across the floor to prove her words. "And this is important. I want to see someone at the hotel."

"So late at night?"

"It really is important," Penny declared. "Please say I may go."

"Very well," agreed Mrs. Downey reluctantly.

Jake took Penny all the way to the hotel. "Shall I help you inside?" he asked.

"Oh, no," she declined hurriedly. "I'll make it fine from here."

After Jake had driven back up the road, Penny limped around to the back entrance of the hotel. She stood for several minutes staring up at the dark windows of the second floor.

"I believe Ralph Fergus and Harvey Maxwell know plenty about Jasko's disappearance," she thought. "But how to prove it?"

On the parking lot only a few steps away stood the Fergus hotel delivery truck. Penny hobbled over to it, and opened the rear door. She swept the beam of her flashlight over the floor.

At first glance the car appeared to be empty save for several cardboard boxes. Then she saw a heavy, fleece-lined glove lying on the floor half hidden by the containers. She picked it up, examined it briefly and stuffed it into the pocket of her snowsuit.

"I remember Peter Jasko wore a glove very much like this!" she thought.

Softly closing the truck door, Penny went back to the rear of the hotel. The lower hall was deserted so she slipped inside, and followed the stairway to the second floor. She tried the door of Room 27 and discovered it was locked.

"I was afraid of this," Penny muttered.

Hesitating a moment she went on down the hall. Opening another door, the one which bore no number, she saw that she was to be blocked again in her investigation. The familiar guard sat at his usual post beside the door of the Green Room.

Retreating without drawing attention to herself, Penny debated her next action. Unless she found a way to enter one of those two rooms of mystery, her night would be wasted.

Moving softly down the hall, she paused to test the door to the right of Room 27. To her astonishment, it swung open when she turned the knob. The room was dark and deserted.

Penny stepped inside, closing the door behind her. Her flashlight beam disclosed only a dusty, bare bedroom, its sole furnishing a thickly padded carpet.

Going to the window, Penny raised it and gazed at the wide ledge which she had noted from below. If she had perfect balance, if the window of Room 27 were unlocked, if her lame ankle did not let her down, she *might* be able to span the distance! It would be dangerous and she must run the risk of being observed by persons on the grounds of the hotel. Penny gazed down at the frozen yard far below and shuddered.

"I've been pretty lucky in my falls so far," she thought. "But I have a feeling if I slip this time it will be my last."

Penny pulled herself through the window. As the full force of the wind struck her body, threatening to hurl her from her precarious perch, she nearly lost her courage. She clung to the sill for a moment, and then without daring to look down, inched her way along the ledge.

Reaching the other window in safety, she tried to push it up. For a dreadful instant, Penny was certain she could not. But it gave so suddenly she nearly lost her balance. Holding desperately to the sill, she recovered, and raised the window.

Penny dropped lightly through the opening into the dark room. Pains were shooting through her ankle, but so great was her excitement she scarcely was aware of any discomfort.

She flashed her light about the room. As she had suspected, there were two teletype machines, neither of which was in operation. A chair had been pulled up to a direct-keyboard machine similar to one Penny had seen in her father's newspaper office. Save for a wooden table the room contained nothing else.

Penny went over to the machines and focused her light upon the paper in the rollers. It was blank.

"This is maddening!" she thought. "I take a big risk to get in here and what do I find—nothing!"

Footsteps could be heard coming down the hallway. Penny remained perfectly still, expecting the person to pass on. Instead, the noise ceased altogether and a key grated in the door lock.

In panic, Penny glanced frantically about. She could not hope to get out the window in time to escape detection. The only available hiding place was a closet.

Switching off her light, Penny opened the door. Stepping inside, she closed it softly behind her.

***

CHAPTER 22

THE SECRET STAIRS

In the darkness, Penny felt something soft and covered with fur brush against her face. She recoiled, nearly screaming in terror. Recovering her poise and realizing that she had merely touched a garment which hung in the closet, she flattened herself against the wall and waited.

The outside door opened and soft footsteps approached the wall switches. Lights flashed on. A tall, swarthy man in a gray business suit blinked at the sudden flood of illumination. After a moment he stepped over to the teletype machines, and throwing a switch, started them going.

Sitting down to the keyboard he tapped out a message. Then he lit a cigarette and waited. In a few minutes his answer came, typed out from some distant station. The man ripped the copy from the machine and read it carefully. Its contents seemed to please him for he smiled broadly as he arose from the chair, leaving the teletypes still running.

Penny froze with fear when she heard the man stride toward the closet where she had hidden herself. Instinctively, she burrowed back behind the fur garments which her groping hands encountered.

The door was flung open and light flooded into the closet. However, the teletype attendant seemed to have no suspicion that anyone might be hiding there. He pressed a button on the wall and then heaved against the partition with his shoulder. The section of wall, suspended on a pivot, slowly revolved. After the man had passed through, it swung back into its original position.

Penny waited several minutes and then came out of her hiding place. She flung open the closet door to admit more light.

"Just as I thought!" she muttered.

The closet, a long narrow room, was hung solidly with fur coats!

"So Maxine Miller was working for the hotel interests after all," Penny told herself. "I've stumbled into something big!"

Groping along the wall of the storage room, she found a switch and pressed it. Again the partition revolved, revealing a flight of stairs leading downward. She slipped through and the wall slid into place behind her.

The stairway was lighted with only one weak electric bulb. Penny's body cast a grotesque shadow as she cautiously descended. There were so many steps that she decided they must lead to a basement in the hotel.

She reached the bottom at last and followed a narrow sloping tunnel, past a large refrigerated vault which she reasoned must contain a vast supply of additional furs, and kept on until a blast of cool air struck her face. Penny drew up sharply.

Directly ahead, at a bend in the tunnel, sat an armed guard. He was reading a newspaper in the dim light, holding it very close to the glaring bulb above his chair.

Penny dared go no farther. Quietly retreating the way she had come, she stole back up the long stairway. At the top landing she found herself confronted with a blank wall. After groping about for several minutes, her hand encountered a tiny switch similar to the one on the opposite side of the partition. She pressed it, and the wall section revolved.

Letting herself out of the storage closet, Penny started toward the door, only to pause as she heard one of the teletypes thumping out a message. She crossed over to the machine and stood waiting until the line had been finished and a bell jingled. The words were unintelligible in jumbled typewriting, and Penny had no time to work out the code.

Tearing the copy paper neatly across, she thrust it in the pocket of her jacket.

Fearing that at any moment the printer attendant might return, Penny dared linger no longer. She went to the door but to her surprise it would not open.

"Probably a special trick catch which automatically locks whenever closed," she thought. "The only way to get in or out is with a key, and I haven't one. That means I'll have to risk my neck again."

Going to the window she raised it and looked down. All was clear below. Two courses lay open to her. She could return the way she had come through the hotel, or she might edge along the shelf past two other windows to the fire escape, and thence to the ground. Either way was fraught with danger.

"If I should happen to meet Ralph Fergus or Harvey Maxwell, I might not get away with my information," Penny decided. "I'll try the fire-escape."

Closing the window behind her, she flattened herself along the building wall, and moved cautiously along the ledge. She passed the first room in safety. Then, as she was about to crawl past the second, the square of window suddenly flared with light.

For a dreadful moment Penny thought that she had been seen. She huddled against the wall and waited. Nothing happened.

At last, regaining her courage, she dared to peep into the lighted room. Two men stood with their backs to the window, but she recognized them as Harvey Maxwell and Ralph Fergus.

Penny received a distinct shock as her gaze wandered to the third individual who sat in a chair by the bed. The man was old Peter Jasko.

A low rumble of voices reached the girl's ears. Harvey Maxwell was speaking:

"Well, Jasko, have you thought it over? Are you ready to sign the lease?"

"I'll have the law on you, if I ever get out of here!" the old man said spiritedly. "You're keepin' me against my will."

"You'll stay here, Jasko, until you come to your senses. We need that land, and we mean to have it. Understand?"

"You won't get me to sign, not if you keep me here all night," Mr. Jasko muttered. "Not if you keep me a year!"

"You may change your mind after you learn what we can do," said Harvey Maxwell suavely.

"You aim to starve me, I reckon."

"Oh, no, nothing so crude as that, my dear fellow. In fact, we shall treat you most kindly. Doctor Corbin will be here presently to examine you."

"Doctor Corbin! That old quack from Morgantown! What are you bringing him here for?"

Harvey Maxwell smiled and tapped his head significantly.

"To give you a mental examination. You are known to the good people of Pine Top as a very peculiar fellow, so I doubt if anyone will question Doctor Corbin's verdict."

"You mean, you're aimin' to have me adjudged insane?" Peter Jasko asked incredulously.

"Exactly. How else can one explain your fanatical hatred of skiing, your blind rages, your antagonism to the more progressive interests? While it will be a pity to bring disgrace upon your charming granddaughter, there is no other way."

"Not unless you decide to sign," added Ralph Fergus. "We're more than reasonable. We're willing to pay you a fair price for the lease, more than the land is worth. But we want it, see? And what we want we take."

"You're a couple of thievin', stealin' crooks!" Peter Jasko shouted.

"Not so loud, and be careful of your words," Harvey Maxwell warned. "Or the gag goes on again."

"Which do you prefer," Fergus went on. "A tidy little sum of money, or the asylum?"

Peter Jasko maintained a sullen silence, glaring at the two hotel men.

"The doctor will be here at ten-thirty," said Harvey Maxwell, looking at his watch. "You will have less than a half hour to decide."

     Behind the Green Door

"My mind's made up now! You won't get anyone to believe your cock and bull story. I'll tell 'em you brought me here and held me prisoner—"

"And no one will believe you," smiled Maxwell. "We'll give out that you came to the hotel and started running amuck. Dozens of employes will confirm the story."

"For that matter, I'm not sure you don't belong in an asylum," muttered Fergus. "Only a man who isn't in his right mind would turn down the liberal proposition we've made you."

"I deal with no scoundrels!" the old man defied them.

Harvey Maxwell looked at his watch again. "You have exactly twenty-five minutes in which to make up your mind, Jasko. We'll leave you alone to think it over."

Fergus trussed up the old man's hands and placed a gag in his mouth. Then the two hotel men left the room, turning out the light and locking the door behind them.

***

CHAPTER 23

RESCUE

After the door had closed there was no further sound for a moment. Then in the darkness Penny heard a choked sob.

Moving closer to the window she tried to raise it. Failing, she tapped lightly on the pane. Pressing her lips close to the glass she called softly:

"Don't be afraid, Mr. Jasko! Keep up your courage! I'll find a way to get you out!"

The old man could not answer so she had no way of knowing whether or not he heard her words. Moving back along the ledge she reached another window, and upon testing it was elated to find that it could be raised up.

She climbed through, lowered it behind her and hastened to the door. Quietly letting herself out, she went down the deserted hall to the next door. Without a key she could not hope to get inside. For a fleeting instant she wondered if she were not making a mistake by delaying in starting after the authorities.

"I never could get back here in time," she told herself. "Maxwell will return in twenty-five minutes with the doctor, possibly earlier. Jasko may sign the paper before help could reach him."

Penny was at a loss to know how to aid the old man. As she stood debating, the cleaning woman whom she had seen upon another occasion, came down the hall. The girl determined upon a bold move.

"I wonder if you could help me?" she said, going to meet the woman. "I've locked myself out of my room. Do you have a master key?"

"Yes, it will unlock most of the bedrooms."

"The doors on this floor?"

"All except number 27."

Penny took a two dollar bill from her jacket pocket and thrust it into the woman's hand.

"Here, take this, and let me have the key."

"I can't give it to you," the woman protested. "Show me your room and I'll unlock it for you."

"We're standing in front of it now. Number 29."

The woman stared. "But these rooms aren't usually given out, Miss."

"I assure you number 29 is very much occupied," replied Penny. "Unlock it, please."

The woman hesitated, and finally inserted the key in the lock.

"Thank you," said Penny as she heard the latch click. "No, keep the two dollars. You are welcome to it."

She waited until the maid had gone on down the hall before letting herself into the dark room. Groping for the electric switch, she turned it on.

"Mr. Jasko, you know me," she whispered as the old man blinked and stared at her almost stupidly. "I'm going to get you out of here."

She jerked the gag from his mouth, and unfastened the cords which bound his wrists.

"We don't dare go through the hotel lest we be seen," she told him. "I think we may be able to get out by means of the fire escape. If luck is only with us—"

Making certain that the coast was clear, Penny led the old man down the hall to a room which she knew would be opposite the fire escape. She was afraid it would be locked, but to her intense relief it had not been secured.

Only a minute was required to cross the room, raise the window and help Peter Jasko through it.

"I can't come with you," she said. "I have something else to do. Now listen closely. I want you to go to Pine Top as fast as you can and bring the sheriff or the police or whoever it is that would have authority to arrest Fergus and Maxwell."

"I aim to do that on my own account," the old man muttered. "I've got a debt to square with them."

"We both have," said Penny. "Now this is what I want you to do. If I'm not in evidence when you get back, bring the police to the Green Room."

"Where's that?"

"It's on this same floor. You go down the hall to the left, enter an unmarked door into another corridor, and finally through a green door which may be guarded. If necessary, force an entrance."

"I don't know what it's all about," the old man muttered. "But I'll do as you say."

"And hurry!" Penny urged.

She watched anxiously from the window until Peter Jasko had reached the bottom of the fire escape in safety. He ran across the yard, gaining the roadway without having been observed.

Returning once more to the main corridor, Penny glanced anxiously up and down. Hearing someone moving about at the far end of the hall, she went to investigate, certain that it was the cleaning woman putting away her mops and broom.

"You ain't locked out again?" the maid asked as she saw Penny standing beside her.

"No, but I have another request. How would you like to earn some more money?"

"How?" inquired the woman with quick interest.

"Do you have an extra costume?"

"Costume?"

"Dress, I mean. Like one you're wearing."

"Not here." As the maid spoke she divested herself of an old pair of shoes, and setting them back against the closet wall, slipped on a pair of much better looking ones. "I'm changing my clothes now to go home."

"I'll give you another two dollars if you'll lend me the outfit for the evening."

"Is it for a party?" the maid asked.

"A masquerade," said Penny. "I want to play a little joke on some acquaintances of mine."

She waved another bill before the woman's eyes, and the temptation of making easy money was too great to resist.

"All right, I'll do it," the maid agreed. "Just wait outside until I get my clothes changed."

Penny waited, watching the halls anxiously lest she be observed by someone who would recognize her. Soon the maid stepped from the closet, and handed over a bundle of clothing.

"And here is your money," said Penny. "Don't mention to anyone what we've done—at least not until tomorrow."

"Don't worry, Miss, I won't," replied the woman grimly. "I might lose my job if they caught me."

After the maid had gone away, Penny slipped into the closet and quickly changed into the costume. Pulling off her cap, she rumpled her hair and rubbed a streak of dirt across her face. The shoes were a trifle too large for her, and their size, together with the painful ankle, made her walk in a dragging fashion.

Snatching up a feather duster, she went hurriedly down the hall toward the corridor which led to the Green Room. As always, the guard sat in his chair by the door. But this time Penny had high hopes of gaining entrance.

Boldly, she walked over to him and said: "Good evening. I was sent to tell you you're wanted in the office by Mr. Maxwell."

"Now?" he inquired in surprise.

"Yes, right away."

"Someone ought to stay here."

"I'll wait until you get back."

"Don't let anyone inside unless they have passes," the guard instructed.

Penny barely could hide her excitement. It had been almost too easy! At last she was to penetrate beyond the Green Door! And if she found what she expected, the entire mystery would be cleared up. She would gain evidence against Ralph Fergus and Harvey Maxwell which would make her case iron-clad.

From within the room, Penny could hear the low murmur of voices. She waited until the guard had disappeared, and then, summoning her courage, opened the green door and stepped inside.

Penny found herself in an elegantly furnished salon, its chairs, davenports, carpet and draperies decorated in soft shades of green and ivory. A little dark-haired man she had never seen before, who spoke with an artificial French accent, stood talking with three women who were trying on fur coats. A fourth woman, Maxine Miller, sat in a chair, her back turned to Penny.

"Now Henri, I want you to give my friends a good price on their coats," she was saying in a chirpy voice.

"*Oui*" he agreed, bobbing his head up and down. "We say one hundred and ninety-two dollars for zis beautiful sealskin coat. I make you a special price only because you are friends of Mademoiselle Miller."

The opening of the outside door had drawn Henri's attention briefly to Penny. As she busied herself dusting, he paid her no heed, and Maxine Miller did not give the girl a second glance.

Penny wandered slowly about the room, noting the long mirrors and the tall cases crowded with racks of sealskin coats.

"These are smuggled furs," she thought. "This Green Room is the sales salon, and Henri must be an employee of Ralph Fergus and Harvey Maxwell. I believe I know how they get the furs over the Canadian border, too, without paying duty!"

Satisfied that she could learn no more by lingering, Penny turned down the long corridor leading to the door which opened on the main hallway. She knew that the guard would soon discover he had been tricked and expose her. And while she had been inside the salon less than five minutes, already she had waited a moment too long.

As she opened the door she saw Harvey Maxwell and the guard coming down the corridor toward her. Retreat was out of the question.

"There she is now!" said the guard, accusingly. "She told me you wanted me in the office."

Harvey Maxwell walked angrily toward Penny.

"What was the big idea?" he began, only to stop short. "Oh, so it's *you*? My dear little girl, I am very much afraid, you have over-played your hand this time!"

***

CHAPTER 24

HENRI'S SALON

Penny sought to push past the two men, but Harvey Maxwell caught her roughly by the arm.

"Unfortunately, my dear Miss Parker, you have observed certain things which you may not understand," he said. "Lest you misinterpret them, and are inclined to run to your father with fantastic tales, you must be detained here. Now I have a great distaste for violence. I trust it will not be necessary to use force now."

"Let me go," Penny cried, trying to jerk away.

"Take her, Frank," instructed the hotel man. "For the time being put her in the tunnel room. I'll be down as soon as I talk with Ralph."

Before Penny could scream, a hand was clapped over her mouth. The guard, Frank, held her in a firm grip from which she could not free herself.

"Get going!" he commanded.

But Penny braced her feet and stood perfectly still. From the outside corridor she had heard a low rumble of voices. Then Ralph Fergus spoke above the others, in an exasperated, harassed tone:

"This old man is crazy, I tell you! We never kept him a prisoner in our hotel. We have a Green Room, to be sure, but it is rented out to a man named Henri Croix who is in the fur business."

Penny's pulse quickened. Peter Jasko had carried out her order and had brought the police!

Harvey Maxwell and the guard well comprehended their danger. With a quick jerk of his head the hotel man indicated a closet where Penny could be secreted. As the two men tried to pull her to it, she sunk her teeth into Frank's hand. His hold over her mouth relaxed for an instant, but that instant was enough. She screamed at the top of her lungs.

The outside door swung open. Led by Peter Jasko, the sheriff and several deputies filed into the corridor. Ralph Fergus did not follow, and Penny saw him trying to slip away.

"Don't let that man escape!" she cried. "Arrest him!"

Peter Jasko himself overtook Fergus and brought him back.

"I've got a score to settle with you," he muttered. "You ain't a good enough talker to get out of this."

"Gentlemen—" It was Harvey Maxwell who spoke, and his tone was irritated. "What is the meaning of this intrusion?"

"We've had a complaint," said the sheriff. "Jasko here says you kept him a prisoner in the hotel, trying to make him sign a paper."

"The old fellow is right in a way," replied Mr. Maxwell. "Not about the paper. We did detain him here for his own good, and he managed to get away. I regret to say he went completely out of his mind, became violent, threatened our guests, and it was necessary to hold him until the doctor could arrive. We've already sent for Doctor Corbin."

"That's just what I was telling them," added Ralph Fergus.

"Now let me speak my piece," said Penny. "Peter Jasko was held a prisoner here because Fergus and Maxwell wanted him to sign a paper leasing his ski slopes to the hotel. That was only one of their many little stunts. Fergus and Maxwell are the heads of a gigantic fur smuggling business, and they use their hotels merely as a legitimate front."

"Your proof?" demanded Harvey Maxwell sarcastically. "The real truth is that I am suing this girl's father for libel. He sent her here to try to dig up something against me. She's using every excuse she can find to involve me in affairs about which I know nothing."

"If you want proof, I'll furnish it," said Penny. "Just step into the Green Room where Henri Croix, a phony Frenchman, is engaged in selling fur coats to three ladies."

"There's no crime in that," declared Ralph Fergus angrily. "Mr. Croix pays the hotel three hundred dollars a month for the use of this wing. So far as we know his business is legitimate. If for any reason we learn it is not, we will be the first to ask for an investigation."

"Not quite the first," smiled Penny, "for I've already made the request. To go on with my proof, it might be well to investigate Room 27 on this same floor."

"Room 27 is given over to our teletype service," interrupted Maxwell. "Our guests like to get the stock reports, you know, and that is why we have the machines."

"In Room 27 you will find a storage vault for furs," Penny went on, thoroughly enjoying herself. "A panel revolves, opening the way to a secret stair which leads down into the basement of the hotel. I'm not certain about the rest—"

"No?" demanded Maxwell ironically.

"There are additional storage vaults in the basement," Penny resumed. "A man is down there guarding what appears to be a tunnel. Tell me, is this hotel close to the old silver mine?"

"About a quarter of a mile from the entrance," replied the sheriff. "Some of the tunnels might come right up to the hotel grounds."

"I understand the hotel bought out the mine, and I believe they may be making use of the old tunnels. At least, the place will bear an investigation. Oh, yes, this paper came off one of the teletype machines."

Penny took the torn sheet from her pocket and gave it to the sheriff.

"I can't read it," he said, frowning.

"Code," explained Penny. "If I had a typewriter I could figure it out. Suppose we go to Room 27 now. I'm positive you'll learn that my story is not as fantastic as it seems."

Leaving Peter Jasko and two deputies to guard Fergus and Maxwell and to see that no one left the Green Room, Penny led the sheriff and four other armed men down the hall. In her excitement she failed to observe Francine Sellberg standing by the elevator, watching intently.

"Here are the teletype machines," Penny indicated, pausing beside them. "Now let me have that message. I think I can read it."

Studying the keyboard of the teletype for a moment, she wrote out her translation beneath the jumbled line of printing. It read:

"Train Arrives approximately 11:25."

"What does that mean?" the sheriff inquired. "We have no trains at Pine Top."

"We'll see," chuckled Penny.

She showed the men the vault filled with furs, and pressed the spring which opened the wall panel.

"Be careful in descending the stairway," she warned. "I know they have one guard down there and possibly others."

Sheriff Clausson and his men went ahead of Penny. The guard, taken completely by surprise, was captured without a shot being fired.

"Now what have we here?" the sheriff inquired, peering into the dimly lighted tunnel.

As far as one could see stretched a narrow, rusted track with an extra rail.

"A miniature electric railway!" exclaimed the sheriff.

"How far is it from here to the border?" inquired Penny thoughtfully.

"Not more than a mile."

"I've been told Harvey Maxwell has a hotel located in Canada."

"Yeah," nodded the sheriff, following her thought. "We've known for years that furs were being smuggled, but we never once suspected the outfit was located here at Pine Top. And no wonder. This scheme is clever, so elaborate a fellow never would think of it. The underground railroad, complete with drainage pumps, storage rooms and electric lights, crosses the border and connects with the Canadian hotel. Fergus and Maxwell buy furs cheap and send them here without paying duty."

"And teletype communication is maintained just as it is on a real railroad," added Penny. "Fergus and Maxwell must have bought up the old mine just so they could make use of the tunnels. And they wanted to get rid of Mrs. Downey's Inn so there would be no possible danger of a leak. How large do you suppose the smuggling ring is, Mr. Clausson?"

"Large enough. Likely it will take weeks to get all of the guilty persons rounded up. But I'm satisfied we have the main persons."

"If I interpreted the code message right, a fur train should be coming in about eleven-thirty."

"My men will be waiting," the sheriff said grimly. "I'll get busy now and tip off the Canadian authorities, so they can close in on the gang from the other end of the line."

"What about Fergus and Maxwell?" asked Penny. "There's no chance they can trump up a story and get free?"

"Not a chance," returned the sheriff gruffly. "You've done your work, and now I'll do mine."

Penny started to turn away, then paused. "Oh, may I ask a favor?"

"I reckon you've earned it," the sheriff answered, a twinkle in his eye.

"There's one person involved in this mess who isn't really to blame. An actress named Maxine Miller. She's only been working for the hotel a few days, and I doubt if she knows what it's all about."

"We'll give her every benefit of the doubt," promised the sheriff. "I'll remember the name. Miller."

In a daze of excitement Penny rushed back up the stairway to the Green Room. Fergus and Maxwell, Henri Croix, and Maxine Miller were in custody, all angrily protesting their innocence. The commotion had brought many hotel guests to the scene. Questions were flying thick and fast.

Penny drew Peter Jasko aside to talk with him privately.

"I think you ought to go to Mrs. Downey's lodge as soon as you can," she urged. "Sara is there, and she's dreadfully worried about you."

"I'll go now," the old man said, offering his gnarled hand. "Much obliged for all you done tonight."

"That's quite all right," replied Penny. "I was lucky or I never would have discovered where those men were keeping you."

The old man hesitated, obviously wishing to say something more, yet unable to find the words.

"I done some thinkin' tonight," he muttered. "I reckon I been too strict with Sara. From now on maybe I'll let her have a looser rein."

"And ski all she likes," urged Penny. "I really can't see the harm in it."

"I been thinkin' about that lease, too," the old man added, not looking directly at the girl. "When I see Mrs. Downey tonight I'll tell her I'm ready to sign."

"Oh, I'm so glad!" Penny exclaimed. "With the Fergus-Maxwell hotel out of the running, she ought to have a comfortable time of it here on Pine Top mountain."

"Thanks to you," grinned Peter Jasko. He offered his hand again and Penny gave it a firm pressure.

"I must hurry now," she said. "This is a tremendous story, and I want to telegraph it to Dad before Francine Sellberg beats me to the jump."

"Sellberg?" repeated the old man. "She ain't that girl reporter that's been stayin' here at the hotel?"

Penny nodded.

"Then you better step," he advised. "She's on her way to the village now."

"But how could Francine have learned about it so soon?" Penny wailed in dismay.

"I saw her talking with one of the deputies. She was writing things down in a notebook."

"She couldn't have learned everything, but probably enough to ruin my story. When did Francine leave, Mr. Jasko?"

"All of fifteen minutes ago."

"Then I never can overtake her," Penny murmured. "This is absolutely the worst break yet! Francine will reach the telegraph office first and hold the wire so I can't use it. After all my work, her paper will get the big scoop!"

***

<h1 align="center">CHAPTER 25</h1>

<h2 align="center">SCOOP!</h2>

Penny knew that she had only one chance of getting her story through to Riverview, and that was by means of long distance telephone. At best, instead of achieving a scoop as she had hoped, she would have only an even break with her rival. And if connections could not be quickly made, she would lose out altogether.

Hastily saying goodbye to Peter Jasko, Penny raced for the stairway. She did not have a word of her story written down. While she could give the facts to a rewrite man it would take him some time to get the article into shape.

"Vic Henderson writes such colorless stories, too," she moaned to herself. "He'll be afraid some fact isn't accurate and he'll jerk it out. This is the one yarn I want to write myself!"

Penny ran full tilt into Sheriff Clausson. She brought up shortly, observing that he had a prisoner in custody.

"Miss Parker, we caught this fellow down in the tunnel," he said. "Can you identify him?"

"I'm not sure of his name. He works for Fergus and Maxwell as a teletype attendant. He may be George Jewitt."

Penny started to hasten on, and then struck by a sudden idea, paused. Addressing the prisoner she demanded:

"Isn't it true that there is a direct wire connection between this hotel and the one in Riverview?"

The man did not speak.

"You may as well answer up," said the sheriff. "It's something which can be checked easily."

"Yes, there is a direct connection," answered the attendant.

"And if I know anything about leased wires," continued Penny with mounting excitement, "it would be possible to have the telephone company switch that wire right over to the *Riverview Star* office. Then I'd have a direct connection from here to the newspaper. Right?"

"Right except for one minor detail," the man retorted sarcastically. "The telephone company won't make a switch just to oblige a little girl."

Penny's face fell. "I suppose they wouldn't do it," she admitted. "But what a whale of an idea! I could send my story directly to the newspaper, and get my scoop after all. As it is, the *Record* is almost certain to beat me."

"Listen!" said the sheriff. "Maybe the telephone company couldn't make the switch on your say-so, but they'll pay attention to an order from me. You get busy writing that story, young lady, and we'll see what can be done."

Sheriff Clausson turned his prisoner over to a deputy, and returned to find Penny busily scribbling on the back of an envelope, the only writing paper available. Together they went to the long distance telephone, and in a quicker time than the girl had dared hope, arrangements were made for the wire shift to be made.

"Now get up to Room 27 and start your story going out," the sheriff urged. "Will you need the attendant to turn on the current for you?"

"No, I know how it's done!" Penny declared. "You're sure the connection has been made?"

"The telephone company reports everything is set. So go to it!"

Penny hobbled as fast as her injured ankle would permit to Room 27. She switched on the light, and turned on the current which controlled the teletype machines. Sitting down at a chair in front of the direct keyboard, she found herself trembling from excitement. She had practiced only a few times and was afraid she might make mistakes.

                                              Behind the Green Door

Every word she wrote would be transmitted in exactly that form to a similar machine stationed in the *Star* office.

She could picture her father standing there, waiting, wondering what she would send. He had been warned that a big story was coming.

Penny consulted her envelope notes and began to tap the keys. Now and then she had moments of misgiving, wondering if her work was accurate, and if it were going through. She finished at last, and sat back with a weary sigh of relief. Her story was a good one. She knew that. But had it ever reached the *Star* office?

A machine to her right began its rhythmical thumping. Startled, Penny sprang to her feet and rushed over to see the message which was slowly printing itself across the copy paper.

"STORY RECEIVED OK. WONDERFUL STUFF. CAN YOU GET AN INTERVIEW WITH SHERIFF CLAUSSON?"

Penny laughed aloud, and went back to her own machine to tap out an answer. Her line had a flippant note:

"I'LL HAUL HIM UP HERE AS SOON AS THE 11:30 TRAIN COMES IN. LET ME TALK TO DAD."

There was a little wait and then the return message came in over the other teletype.

"YOU'VE BEEN TALKING WITH HIM. AM SENDING SALT SOMMERS BY PLANE TO GET PICTURES. SORRY I DIDN'T TAKE YOU SERIOUSLY WHEN YOU WROTE MAXWELL WAS INVOLVED IN ILLEGAL BUSINESS AT PINE TOP. THIS OUGHT TO MOP UP HIS SUIT AGAINST THE PAPER. GREAT STUFF, PENNY! WHO UNCOVERED THE STORY?"

Chuckling to herself, Penny went back to her keyboard and tapped:

"DON'T ASK ME. I'M TRYING TO BE MODEST."

She waited eagerly for the response and it came in a moment.

"I WAS AFRAID OF IT. ARE YOU ALL RIGHT?"

Thoroughly enjoying the little game of questions and answers, Penny once more tapped her message.

"FINE AS SILK. WHEN ARE YOU COMING TO PINE TOP? WHAT ARE YOU GOING TO GIVE ME FOR XMAS? IT SHOULD BE SOMETHING GOOD AFTER THIS."

Soon Mr. Parker's reply appeared on the moving sheet of paper.

"SOON. PERHAPS SOMETHING WITH FOUR WHEELS AND A HORN."

Penny scarcely could control herself long enough to send back:

"OH, YOU WONDERFUL DAD! I COULD HUG YOU! PLEASE MAKE IT MAROON WITH MOHAIR UPHOLSTERY. AND HANG A WREATH ON LEAPING LENA."

Sinking back in her chair, Penny gazed dreamily at the ceiling. A new car! It was almost too good to believe. She knew that her father must have been swayed by excitement or else very grateful to offer such a magnificent Christmas present as that. What a night of thrills it had been! Within a few hours Pine Top would be crowded with reporters and photographers, but she had uncovered the story, and had saved her father from a disastrous lawsuit.

As Penny waited, her thoughts far away, one more message came through on the teletype. She tore it from the roller of the machine, and smiled as she read her father's final words:

"PRESSES ROLLING. FIRST EDITION ON THE STREET AHEAD OF THE RECORD. THE STAR SCORES AGAIN. THIS IS ANTHONY PARKER SIGNING OFF FOR A CUP OF COFFEE."

THE END.

www.ingramcontent.com/pod-product-compliance
Lightning Source LLC
LaVergne TN
LVHW051534170726
843492LV00006B/1770